ISBN 978-0-578-51490-1

www.geminicblue.com

To my family, to Spyn, Tiffany, and two Kims, to

Ms. Martin, Amanda and Molly, and everyone who has

followed this story online for the past two decades

To everyone who believed in me when I did not

Table of Contents

Chapter 1 ★ ★ ★ Freezing Rain

A murmur of thunder woke Ru from heavy sleep. It was only a whisper in her ear, but she sat up and threw off her blanket, ignoring the chill air. She rushed to the window and shoved the dark curtains aside. The first thing she did every morning was look at the sky, but rarely with such energy.

The maple and birch trees along Plover Road were in a frenzy, the sky dim and the slate clouds bulging. Lightning stabbed down at rows of houses. Ru jumped into her T-shirt and jeans and tore down the stairs. Still at top speed, she grabbed a bowl of cereal, then bolted to the living room and slid in front of the TV. Her mother had left the news on.

The weatherman, in a brown corduroy suit that seemed decades too old for him, pointed and waved over a blotchy map of northern Illinois. A Severe Thunderstorm Warning, in effect for the entire station viewing area. Corduroy Man mentioned the squall line would likely pass north of Quarterhill, but Ru knew from her glance out the window that she would still see quite a storm.

Ru's mother watched from behind the kitchen counter. "Be careful out there. No missing the bus to walk in the rain."

"What? But I want to see --"

Her mother cut her off. "I don't want you getting caught in a hailstorm. Or being late for class."

"But Mooom," Ru whined.

"This kind of weather is dangerous." There was a note of warning in her mother's voice that had more to do with patience than with the weather. "How many times do I have to tell you that? Take the bus."

"*Fine.*"

A peculiar silence fell. That was when Ru's younger brother was supposed to make some smart remark. "Where's Jayson? He's going to miss the bus too."

"Jayson's riding with the Fresnels."

Ru was momentarily jealous of Jayson's ride, but if she'd rode with them, she would have to put up with Jayson's annoying friend Randy. She wolfed down the rest of her breakfast and ran out the door. If she couldn't walk in the storm, she'd at least enjoy it before the bus came.

She settled at the corner where Plover met Cardinal and glanced up the sparsely-lit road. It was narrow, chipped and unmarked except for cracks patched with tar. It was hard to believe that further north, Cardinal was one of the busiest roads in Quarterhill. It passed some of the town's most famous sites, like the Breckenridge Mansion and Tanager Park. Ru's best friend Colleen lived at the mansion, and as for Tanager Park, well, every resident of Quarterhill knew it backwards and forwards.

Colleen was supposed to be at the corner, along with several other people. No one was there yet, which was unusual even though Ru had left late. She wondered absently if, despite her mother's best efforts, she'd missed the bus anyway. She peered up the street, up the big hill where Breckenridge was. She could not see the house itself, but the gate always shrieked with age when it was opened. Ru only heard the wind hissing in the trees. A few crows cawed nearby, swaying back and forth on the tops of a towering cottonwood.

Thunder rolled, and the patter of rain followed. Ru tilted her head up and closed her eyes. She felt the fresh wind swirl around her, felt the rain trickle down her face and wash away the last lingering bits of muggy morning sleepiness. She spun on her toes, dancing, laughing, singing. She didn't care if any of her classmates saw her, it was the best morning she'd had in a long time. She felt alive.

Someone was walking down Cardinal. She stopped dancing, not out of embarrassment, but because she couldn't see the person clearly. They were hidden entirely under a red raincoat that reached the ground, with a hood that shrouded their face in shadow. Ru had never seen a coat like that. At first, she considered it was Randy Fresnel trying to pull some quick prank, but even Randy wasn't this short. Still, there was something about this person that sat in Ru's mind the wrong way.

It didn't take long to understand what it was that bothered her. There were no footsteps flashing under the fringes of that coat, no bob of a normal walking rhythm, but the stranger was approaching quickly, at least at a jogger's pace. Rollerblades? Would she be able to hear the wheels over the storm brewing? No, the stranger couldn't have been on wheels. They were slowing as they traveled further down the hill.

They drew closer and closer. The hairs on the back of Ru's neck bristled. The rain on her face felt more like sweat. She stepped out of the way. As the stranger started to cross Plover, the dark opening in the hood twisted towards Ru.

Everything froze.

Ru was alone. The rain speckled the air around her in silvery bubbles. A fork of lightning lay silent across the clouds. The only sounds were her heart thudding her ears and her shoes scraping the pavement as she spun around, frantically trying to make sense what she was seeing. She reached for one of the floating raindrops.

Before her fingers made contact, something tried to push her down, something *big*. It felt like the sky itself suddenly pressed down on her. Her ears swarmed with noise. There were words coded in the rhythm of her heartbeat, words that didn't make sense, so unfamiliar she couldn't even think of how to write them. The pressure reduced her to a hunch. Out of the storm she saw a blinding shaft of light, smoothly weaving, searching, lunging straight for her heart.

She woke with a jolt and a snort. Her head ached from leaning against the bus window. Her stomach roiled, and she wasn't sure if it was from the memory of that light or the fishy smell of the bus seats. Groaning, she rested her head on the scarred vinyl in front of her. She soothed her pounding heart by telling herself she'd had worse nightmares, and there was still a storm to watch. She knew she was back to normal when she wished the stranger hadn't been a dream after all.

Chapter 2 ★ ★ ★ Legends of Quarterhill

It was easier than usual for Ru's class to settle. The morning gloom saturated everything even with the shades drawn. Miss Graham was the only one fully awake, a contagious smile on her face and her hair up in bouncy curls. She almost skipped as she walked to her desk.

Ru wished the shades were open. The day that had started out so well had gone straight downhill after that dream. Colleen never made it to school, there was a Social Studies test Ru had completely forgotten about, and by the time school was out, the storms would be long over. Ru was especially worried about Colleen, who never stayed home from school unless she was very sick.

Miss Graham took her usual place in front of the class after taking attendance. "Today we start the Local Legends unit."

The class burst into smiles and excited whispers. Ru herself suddenly felt far more energized. *Guaranteed A*, she sang in her head.

Miss Graham gestured to a bulletin board. A map of Oak County was posted there, along with several tourist brochures and photos of old buildings and trees. "Can anyone tell me why our town is named Quarterhill?"

A sea of fluttering hands went up. Miss Graham called on Nathan Hall. "Because of the Quarterstone in Tanager Park," he said.

"Very good." Miss Graham beamed. "But the Quarterstone is not the official symbol of our town. What is? Let's see if our new student knows this one. Kenna?"

Kenna shrank in her seat, her voice soft. That was a surprise to Ru. In the few days Kenna had been in the class, she never seemed shy. She would ramble on to anyone that was listen about what it was like to live in Chicago. "The Blue Star?" she answered.

"The Blue Star," Miss Graham echoed. "*Legends of Quarterhill* is coming around now. When you get your copy, turn to Page 31."

Ru grinned as she opened the slender book. There was a painting of a burning blue star floating in a dark wood. She'd seen the painting many times before. Prints of it were sold in Quarterhill stores, and the original painting greeted guests at the Visitor Center on the north end of Tanager Park. The star was even on some of the town limit signs. It always seemed strange to have such an ominous figure welcome tourists, but it was exactly the kind of thing most Tanager Park tourists came to see.

"The artist called it 'a light like the Pleiades.'" Miss Graham lowered her voice, her tone mysterious and musical. The class was silent, all eyes on her. "The Blue Star wanders the woods of Tanager Park at night. It's said that those who cross its path disappear."

By the time the story was finished, Ru had forgotten her previous troubles. The Blue Star was her favorite Quarterhill legend. Everyone had a different way of telling it, and she was never tired of listening. At the same time, the story saddened her a little. The first person who shared it with her was her father.

"You were barely talking when he told you that story," her mother said. "I don't know how you could possibly remember that."

Before Ru could think too much about it, the class started pushing their desks together for a group worksheet. Ru and Nathan usually grouped with Colleen, but Kenna joined them instead. Nathan welcomed her with an awkward smile. "I guess you can work with us. How much do you know about the legends?"

"A little."

Kenna settled back into her desk. She was a tall, lanky girl and the desk was a poor fit, but she made no complaints. She started to open her book. Ru blocked it with the tips of her fingers. "It's OK, we don't need that."

Kenna's gaze skimmed across the clusters of desktops. Only paper and pens could be seen, no open books. "Wow," she breathed. "Daddy said all the kids in this town knew the stories by heart, but I thought he was just trying to get me to do extra credit."

Nathan chewed on the end of his pen. "Just wait until you see they're true."

"They are not," Ru said. "Not all of them."

"Melissa saw the Aurora Pools last week."

"Aurora Pools?" Kenna asked.

"They're like lakes filled with light. People see them in the woods sometimes."

"Oh, come on." Ru rolled her eyes. "Everyone says they see these weird things, but for all we know they were shop owners running around in the woods with flashlights trying to give the tourists something to talk about. Nathan just freaks out a lot because he lives right next to the park."

"So do I," Kenna said uncertainly.

"No one lives that far from it," Nathan said. "Look at the map. The park takes up half the town."

"Have either of you seen the Blue Star?"

"No," Ru and Nathan answered at once, dejected.

Kenna blinked in surprise. "Are there pictures?"

"No one has a good shot of it." Ru opened her book to the painting. "Not a photo of it, anyway. You wouldn't believe how crowded it gets here around Halloween, but no one comes back with pictures or videos, just stories. My brother says, 'If so many people see the star, how are they around to talk about it? Why didn't they disappear?'"

Kenna relaxed a bit. "Good question."

She was in most of Ru's classes, and with each class, Kenna brought up more questions. By the end of the day, Ru agreed to show her around the park on the way home. They set right out for Cardinal Street after the last bell.

Near Quarterhill Middle School, the park was closed off by a half-mile of thick hedges and chain-link fence, but halfway to Ru's house it opened to an expanse of mowed grass. There were teams of older kids already practicing at the baseball and soccer fields. Even though the air was cool, the sun was high in the clear sky and the park glittered with the last of drying rain. The playground and picnic tables were crowded with families out to enjoy the final days of summer warmth. Trains of ringing bicycles and skateboarders coasted down paved paths that wound along the edges of the park.

Ru and Kenna followed a path near the east end. They circled a pond, where flocks of Canada geese murmured as they passed. The path brought them briefly into the woods, the shallow part of the forest where the trees were still young. Mulch veins ran further off into the woods. "If you don't know where you're going, don't take the woodchip trails without a map," Ru warned. "Tourists lose kids in there every couple of months."

"It looks like a normal park to me." Kenna shrugged. "I don't get how people can believe these weird stories." She caught Ru's eye and frowned. "I mean, no offense."

"Oh, no!" Ru laughed. "I totally get what you mean. It's just that when you *have* seen such weird stuff, you don't know what to believe."

"What weird stuff have you seen?"

It was an innocent question, but hearing it gutted Ru. Her mind raced. At last, the silence forced it out of her. "Nothing, actually."

Kenna raised an eyebrow. "Didn't you say you've lived here all your life?"

Ru opened her mouth to reply and was cut off by a rough shout. Normally she would have been annoyed to hear that gravelly voice, but now she was grateful for the interruption.

On the porch of a house across the street, a sour-faced man paced with a limp. His sweatshirt and jeans hung on his bony frame like they would on a scarecrow's, and his stiff, straw-blond hair added to the illusion. Every once in a while he seized the rail and leaned over the side to yell at whoever happened to be passing by. "The tourism board should be locked up, every one of them!" He pointed a thin, gnarled finger at the tops of the trees.

"He's kind of weird," Ru cracked.

Kenna seemed personally offended by the man's rantings. "What's his problem?"

There had been stories told about this man too. Supposedly he had been around since the town's founding, but Ru was sure he wasn't that old. "No idea. Usually he's down at the Main Street shops yelling like that until the cops show up."

"Great. I live two houses away."

She led Ru to the porch of a cute pink and white house that smelled of new concrete. Though Kenna invited

Ru in, Ru said she had too much homework to do. In truth, she was still worried about Colleen, and now that she'd chosen to walk home, she wasn't sure she'd make the Breckenridge visiting hours.

Ru's mood dampened as she jogged home. Kenna's question hung heavy in her mind. *Why not me? Why haven't I ever seen one of the legends? Are they really just stories? Are people lying about what they saw?*

Chapter 3 ★★★ Ruster

Traffic picked up as Ru made her way home. She weaved into drainage ditches to avoid passing cars, ignoring the cool rainwater that trickled through her sneakers and socks. Sparrows chirped, a lawnmower sputtered and roared in a yard across the street, and yet they all seemed miles away. She was lost in the onslaught of questions her mind asked. She didn't notice how close she was to home until a shout sent her thoughts scattering.

"Hey Ruster!"

Ru glared down Plover Road. The Hadley house was second on the street, a two-story tucked away inside a miniature forest of maples, crabapple trees, and blue spruces. Its walls and roof were a dark brown that reminded her of topsoil, with splintering window frames and faded brick accents. A walk made of uneven stones led to a concrete porch. There was a thin petunia garden that followed the edge of the walk and porch. One of Ru's after-school chores was to water the flowers, but she wasn't going anywhere near them with Jayson and Randy sitting on the porch, grinning in the shadows. Her brother she could deal with, but the sight of Randy Fresnel made her want to go back to the park and keep wallowing.

"Don't call me Ruster!" she shouted at them.

"Geez, OK. Sorry, *Prudence*," Jayson shouted back.

The mention of her full name made Ru as prickly as the spruces. She stormed up the driveway and loomed over the two snickering boys. Her looming, as usual, had no effect. Only Jayson's sly grin could be seen under his beloved White Sox cap, the only thing he ever wore that showed a hint of age. He was wearing a new baseball jersey and dark blue jeans without a speck of dirt on them. Randy was the opposite, his clothes riddled with holes and grass stains. He had more bandages crisscrossing his limbs than he had fingers. His hair was vivid red, despite the filth that streaked each short cowlick.

"Don't call me that either," Ru snapped.

"Can we call you Rude?" Randy asked eagerly.

"No."

"Dense?"

"*No!*"

Randy swept away from Ru, his ever-present rollerblades clattering across the front walk stones. "Ruster it is then!"

Ru huffed and stomped into the house as the two boys started singing. They knew far too many songs about roosters as far as she was concerned. "Go home, Randy!" she hollered at him before slamming the door.

"Jayson?" her mother called from upstairs.

"No, he's outside with Randy!"

Ru set her backpack on the kitchen counter and glanced at the clock. As she'd predicted, visiting hours for Breckenridge were over. At least phone calls were accepted until nine. Her mother came down the stairs, wearing far more jewelry than usual and a frilly blouse that reminded Ru of orange pulp. "There you are," she said, giving Ru a quick hug. "I've got some interviews tonight, so I won't be back until late. Kelly's coming by in a little while."

Ru frowned. "I'm twelve, Mom, we don't need a sitter."

"She's just coming by to clean." Her mother gestured to the living room and set an envelope on the counter. "This

is for her. Tell Jayson to come inside when she gets here. I
told her she could bring pizza."

Kelly wasn't really that bad, especially when she
showed up with some of her ultra-cheesy homemade pizzas
to share. She was a college freshman Jayson described as
"stuck in the 80s," citing her neon accessories and huge curly
hairstyle. The problem was she was always coming by to
"clean," but ended up staying long after the house had been
deemed spotless, until whenever Ru's mother just happened
to come home.

The garage door hummed shut, and Ru picked up the
phone. Breckenridge's end had barely begun to ring before it
was scooped up and there was a breathless, "Hello?"

"Hi, is Colleen there?" Ru asked.

An impatient sigh, puffed into the phone. "She can't
talk right now." A muffled, "It's not him" followed.

"Well, is one of the house mothers there?" Ru
persisted. "I have to give Colleen her homework."

"No. She's in the hospital." Someone giggled in the
background, and Ru gritted her teeth as she recognized who
was speaking. "They're not sure if she's going to make it, so I
don't think she's worried about homework right now."

"Shut up and put her on the phone, Ronnie," Ru
growled.

There was a click and a dial tone. Ru slammed the
phone in its cradle and pressed redial. After four tries, she did
manage to give her message to a very irritated house mother,
who confirmed that Colleen was actually sick but was in no
danger.

That done, Ru lugged her backpack to the living
room. Once her eyes adjusted to the dimness, they nearly
bulged out of her head. The shorter of the two couches was

overturned, its blue, flower-speckled cushions in a pile by the fireplace. Paper and mounds of baseball cards blanketed the carpet, and a faint aroma of cooked salami hung in the air next to a pair of saucers slick with brown grease. Most mothers Ru knew would be furious about a mess like this, but a shuffle through some of the papers revealed half of this was Ms. Hadley's own doing. The story about Kelly cleaning was more plausible now.

Ru righted the short couch, then lay back with her head and ankles propped on the armrests and her nose buried in her new textbook. Golden sunlight trickled in through the kitchen patio blinds, illuminating the pages. The myth for the weekly essay was about the Aurora Pools. Before she knew it, she had read through the Legend of the Cameraman, the Angel of Leaves, the Midnight Sun, and the Storm Owl. Her eyes strained for more as the room grew dimmer and dimmer.

A silhouette appeared in the corner of her eye.

It seized her shoulders. Its nails dug through her shirt as it shook her, howling, an unearthly wavering shriek. Ru shrieked back and wrenched away. She scrambled over the armrest and backed up against the wall before recognizing Jayson. His eyes were wide with amusement, gleaming in the deep shadows formed by the brim of his hat. "You didn't even hear me walk in."

Ru threw her book at him. "What is your problem?"

Jayson ducked away. "You want the last can of ravioli?"

"Kelly's bringing food."

"It's seven-thirty already," Jayson pointed out.

With a shock, Ru glanced at the clock on the VCR, then went to the patio door and nudged the shades aside. A pair of stars winked at her from a darkening indigo sky. Her stomach growled loudly, as if it too was just realizing the time.

She stumbled as a head rush momentarily blotted out her vision. The answering machine on the kitchen counter read 0, and Ru could not remember the phone ringing, though to be fair, she hadn't noticed Jayson return to the house as he'd said. "She's usually here by five."

Jayson shrugged. "She got stuck in traffic or something. You want the ravioli or not?"

Ru shook her head and went hunting in the cabinets for her own dinner. "Where'd Randy go?"

Out of the corner of her eye, she saw frustration spread across Jayson's face. "Grounded. Joe Stalvey was messing with him at recess and Randy gave him a black eye."

"He's going to get kicked out of school if he keeps getting into fights." Ru didn't feel all that bad about the prospect.

Exasperation broke through in Jayson's voice. When he was upset, he had a very brisk way of speaking, just like their mother. It made Ru feel like she was the younger sibling. "I know. I keep telling him that, but he doesn't believe me."

"Joe probably deserved it," Ru said. "He'll get kicked out before Randy does."

"Joe was going to prank the new girl in your class."

Although Quarterhill Middle School was fairly large, Ru was not surprised Jayson knew who Kenna was. He had friends in all grades. "You can tell a new kid anything about the park and they believe it."

"Not Kenna." Ru waffled between a can of macaroni and cheese and a small box of cereal. "She asked all the tough questions."

Jayson snorted. "They're only tough for people who believe those stories."

Ru didn't respond. This was not one of the times she found Jayson's cynicism comforting. It was so easy for him to brush the legends off as a marketing ploy, and it was so easy for others to believe every word of the stories was real. Ru felt caught between the two, a lonely place.

Her father had been in the same state of mind. She hadn't realized it until later on. He was looking for proof. She only remembered him in flashes, his smiling face peeking over the top of her stroller on a warm summer night. Her mother had a photograph of the two of them in what Ru was certain was the same moment. He looked like an older version of Jayson, but then again, not. Same inky black hair, same White Sox cap, same pointed chin and small, round nose. On the other hand, his face was full of stubble, his clothes wrinkled and grin uneven. He was a lot more relaxed than her mother, who stood behind the stroller with a dignified smile.

Something flashed.

Ru's heart jumped. There had been a light in the darkest corner of the cabinet, small but too bright to be a simple reflection, almost bright enough to sting her eyes. Static shock? It hadn't touched her, if that was the case.

Another head rush came on, worse than before. She groaned and eased herself away from the counter. Jayson eyed her, but she barely noticed. The shadows over his eyes stood out more, the sharp, curled shadows in the dark rooms around the kitchen. They formed shapes in Ru's spinning head. Her stomach tied in knots. She swallowed hard and tried to get a grip on herself with pure logic. She was probably hungry, or maybe sick. If Colleen was sick, she could have caught it too. She should go lie down. The thought became more and more appealing each second. Not resting or eating, but leaving the room.

Now.

"Jayson." Her voice quivered.

Jayson opened his mouth, but whatever he had to say disappeared in the buzz that filled the room. The sound came from somewhere overhead. A violin, with crooked strings and a bow full of thorns. The louder the sound became, the more pressure Ru felt on the top of her head. Her knees trembled with the effort of standing.

Don't stand. Run.

Jayson stared up at the kitchen light. It seemed ready to burst under the pressure. Ru couldn't tell if he was looking at it because of her, or if he could hear the noise as well. It was hard to tell by his face, eyes wide but not quite alarmed.

A chill streaked up her spine.

Run, her mind screamed. *Now!*

Chapter 4 ★★★ Windsock People

Ru knew her brother could hear the shrill sound when he dropped the empty ravioli can and ran to the living room with her. She scrabbled at the patio door there, but it hadn't been opened in years and neither one of them could remove the safety bar. The two of them scrambled over the side of the sofa and crouched behind the backrest.

Gravity changed course. Every tile in the room clattered, the air in the house pulled, drained towards the kitchen light. Then, a flash -- but not a flash of light. Ru's eyes struggled to focus. It was glowing, but everything it touched changed color instead of lit up. It was as if she was looking at a film negative of the room. Her own skin flushed sickly blue, the shadows of the furniture turned white.

There was something solid in the kitchen when it faded. Two shapes, hovering just below the ceiling. One was gray and long, shaped like a thin tornado, the other looked like a giant burnt marshmallow. They had cat eyes, narrow slit pupils with glowing violet and green irises. The creatures had catlike mouths as well, crinkled skin like the surfaces of a dried lake, and something tilted above the tops of their bodies. A ring, a cold halo.

"A windsock and a marshmallow," Jayson murmured. "Too bad we're dreaming. I could have sold this as one of the legends."

Was there a legend already like it? It had to be a dream, Ru agreed silently, but the thought didn't make her feel any better. Most of her concentration went into keeping her breathing quiet and slow. She was trembling, and she wasn't sure if it was fear or because the room felt so cold. She wanted to wake up and get a thicker blanket.

The gray creature opened its mouth.

The sound tore into Ru's ears like the scream of a jetliner. She and Jayson both hunched and clapped their hands over their ears, but it did nothing to ease the pain. Each syllable the creature pronounced sent a rush of searing needles stabbing through her veins. Her heart struggled to find its own rhythm again, struggled to work at all, as if it were pumping wet cement. She barely noticed the creature had spoken at a normal volume.

The negative light flashed again, and the voice stopped. She sat in a limp ball, stifling sobs. If this was a dream, it was the worst nightmare she'd ever had. She only dared to move again when she heard a human voice. A woman.

"That should take care of it."

Ru and Jayson exchanged glances. Jayson's dark eyes were full of surprise and hurt, but otherwise his face was calm. He peered over the top of the couch again. With all effort to contain her terror, her mind screaming that it was just a dream, Ru eased herself back into a kneel.

Humans stood in place of the floating creatures. One was a pale, shapely woman with silver hair, so shiny it was almost metallic. Split white bangs framed her young face. The other was a tall, square man with hair that looked like an oil slick. He had beady eyes, a vivid enough shade of green for Ru to see a good thirty feet away, and a hard face she couldn't imagine with a smile. Both were dressed in tight black clothing and armor that reminded Ru of SWAT uniforms. The woman wore a belt of square silver plates on her hips.

The woman surveyed the kitchen with narrow eyes, eyes too similar to the form she'd taken a few moments earlier. The way the man followed her every tiny footstep made Ru think she was in charge. He winced slightly when he spoke to her. "Are you sure they're here? It looks empty."

"Maybe they're aliens," Jayson said.

Ru jumped at the sound of his plain-spoken voice. The intruders had to have heard him. Clearly, he'd already forgotten what pain a simple dream could put him through. "Get down!" she hissed. "They'll see you!"

Before the last word left her lips, a shadow fell over them. Ru shrieked and nearly slipped off the couch. The woman, in less than half a second, had crossed that thirty feet of space without a footstep. Jayson's eyes widened, but he stayed upright, even showing a hint of defiance. The woman's expression, however, softened into an excited smile. "Crowe, look! Children. How cute!"

Jayson became more than defiant now, indignant. Ru almost relaxed, but when Crowe joined his partner, she understood letting her guard down was a very bad idea. His scorn was directed at the woman, though. "Sylph. Sylph!" He reached for her shoulder, then thought better of touching her and waved his hand in front of her face. "This could be a trap."

"Why are they afraid of us?" Sylph wondered absently.

"It *is* the sleeping planet."

Jayson barked a laugh. "Please. I'm not afraid of you."

Ru watched her brother out of the corner of her eye and tried to resist curling into a ball again. It didn't seem like he was being very smart, but it was a dream. Wasn't it? Ru wasn't so sure anymore. She tried everything to wake herself up. She purposely scrambled her thoughts. She pinched her own arm. She tried falling asleep, as impossible as that seemed.

"No?" Sylph said.

Jayson tipped the bill of his cap up. "I've had scarier dreams than this."

She looked on the verge of a laughing fit. "Dreams?"

"Yeah." Jayson crossed his arms. "You can't be real. Giant living windsocks and marshmallows -- I won't even tell you what's wrong with *that* -- can't turn into people."

"Jayson, let the windsock people turn into whatever they want!" Ru squeaked.

A threatening look flashed across Crowe's face. Jayson made a mistake, Ru realized, mentioning he'd seen the alien forms of the intruders. She felt queasy with terror. Crowe forced Sylph aside and held his hand in an upturned claw, straining as if he was trying to lift a heavy door. "I don't care what they are," he growled. "They've seen too much."

Green fire burst from his palm. The sickly flames forced into a ball. There was no smoke, but a distinct stench filled the room and froze Ru in place. She felt cold and hollow, like the entire universe had been emptied except for her. Sylph stood calmly aside. She would not step in.

It's a dream, Ru thought again. The words were as empty as Crowe's flames. The fire did nothing to his gloves, but as the fireball grew it stung Ru's skin like a bad sunburn. She couldn't back away, she'd forgotten how. The green light of the fire filled the room, turning the quaint garden wallpaper into a toxic wasteland. Then the light went cyan, then blue. The flames lashed out, eager to be released, to consume.

The blue light. It wasn't coming from the flames. It was shining behind Sylph.

"*Look out!*" Sylph screamed. Crowe had just enough time to turn his head.

A brilliant torrent of blue-white light blasted out of the kitchen. Wind roared through the house. The floor rumbled as if a train was passing through. Papers fluttered into the air. That horrible rasping voice tore from Crowe's throat in an agonized scream, but its effects were nullified by the sound of the light. The alien man became a silhouette as the light ripped into him. He was shredded, faded as he lost form. For a moment, Ru thought she saw a bird, a crow flapping its wings before it winked out of sight.

The light merely passed over everything else it touched. It packed into a solid point, a ball that shined like the sun, only blue. Four delicate beams formed a cross from its center. Soft tendrils of cerulean flame flowed around its edges.

When Ru finally realized what she was looking at, her fears tripled. If the aliens didn't fry her, she and Jayson would certainly be lost to the Blue Star.

Sylph's arms were raised defensively, her teeth bared. "What are *you* doing here?"

"Leave immediately, or you will share the same fate as your guard."

Ru felt fear momentarily give way to surprise. The Star's voice was sweet and clear, the sound of wind chimes in the breeze. Most legends did not have the Star speak, but those that did told of its ferocious, howling voice, all the thunder of a storm contained in a few words. Maybe this wasn't the Blue Star, but Ru couldn't think of anything else it would be.

Sylph gaped at the Star, then at Ru and Jayson, and her expression changed several times in a few moments. Confusion, realization, and a deadly glare aimed squarely at the two children. Ru wanted to wither up at that. Then the negative light flashed again, and Sylph was gone.

They sat absolutely still. Ru heard Jayson's breathing, soft and even, but he was shaking.

Here they were, facing a legend. The very symbol of their town and the unknown, the Blue Star. It was looking at them. Ru didn't know how she could tell, it didn't have a face, but she knew.

"Please do not fear me," it chimed. "Though many have vanished before me, I will bring you no harm."

Its crystalline voice sounded like a mobile. The way the fire flickered gently around its edges brought heaviness to Ru's mind. She set her head on the backrest of the couch, and found the dreamless sleep she was looking for.

Chapter 5 ★ ★ ★ Dreams

Everything was light. Air bright as the sun, flowing like feathers on the wind. Weight was not relevant, substance less so, only the shine. Sleep was the lightest of all.

Ru sat up in bed, buzzing with so much energy she felt like she could fly. Her imagination painted fiery aliens and Blue Stars behind everything she couldn't see through. Slowly, she wormed her way across her bed and inched the heavy blue curtains open. The branches of the big maple out front were still, save for the silhouettes of fluttering birds. The sky was dim, clear, and rosy.

Did Jayson have the same dream? He hated mornings, so it would be a challenge to get him to talk. Upon reaching the kitchen, she found him in a worse state than usual. He was practically face-down in his cereal. His ratty hat obscured his face. She never saw his eyes once before they left the house, and he answered her questions in grunts or single words. "I don't remember my dreams," he said gruffly. He left for the bus stop early, and by the time she got to the corner, Randy and Vince Faraday were already there. The three boys shut Ru out of their conversation.

The gate up the street squealed, and a minute later, a train of girls in pleated navy dresses marched to the corner. Colleen, who was taller than all her housemates by a head, was not among them. The girls formed another closed circle when they reached the stop. Alone, Ru watched Jayson with a sour face and listened to them argue about baseball.

Once on the bus, Jayson went for the back rows with Vince. Ru didn't bother following. The eighth-graders in those seats would give her the evil eye for even approaching that part of the bus. Jayson was the only one in the lower

grades deemed worthy to sit with the senior class. He even
left Randy behind, who resorted to torturing the
Breckenridge girls with a crushed Hostess cupcake he'd found
in his backpack.

The bus screeched to a halt just after starting and
opened the doors again. Ru perked up when she saw a head
of long pale hair with a pink headband bob past her window.
The Breckenridge girls groaned collectively and snickered
amongst themselves. No doubt they were the ones that made
Colleen late, but Ru wasn't in the mood to tangle with them.
Everything else in her mind was crowded out by that dream.

As soon as Colleen took the seat across the aisle, Ru
spilled the entire story, Blue Star, aliens, and all. Colleen
listened without question or reaction. Her eyelids drooped,
her face long and weary. Her uniform was wrinkled, though
clean, the triangular Breckenridge patch on the front still the
whitest of whites and jarring red, depicting a nuthatch and a
pine branch in clean embroidery. The only thing that shined
on her was the dolphin pendant she always wore. Colleen
tugged at her tie and took deep breaths every time the bus
jumped. "Are you OK?" Ru asked.

Afterwards, there was silence between them until they
reached school. The girls walked down the hall side-by-side,
as much as the crowds would allow. Colleen's eyes lingered
on the floor. Her question just barely reached Ru over the
clang of shutting lockers and idle chatter. "Is Kelly all right?"

"All right?" Ru echoed, raising an eyebrow. "She
never showed up last night. Mom called her this morning, but
I didn't hear what she was saying."

"I had a dream."

Ru's eyes widened, and she drew in closer. "One of
those dreams?"

Colleen nodded. Her face made her ordinary expression look as bright as a summer noon. "She was in a car accident. She lost an eye. The dream made me sick. I wasn't here yesterday because they thought I had the stomach flu."

She still sounded sick, and Ru was beginning to feel it. Ms. Hadley hadn't indicated any of this, but when Ru measured her mother's reactions and answers on the phone that morning, it all fit. "Does she live?" Ru asked quietly.

Tears welled up in Colleen's eyes, but she nodded. The dreams Colleen had rarely involved anyone either one of them knew, which was fortunate because most of them terrified Colleen into screaming herself awake. Worse, Colleen was certain all the dreams came true. They had only found evidence a few times, but Colleen said that in many of them the people involved spoke languages she did not recognize or understand.

Colleen had vivid dreams normally, but she said these were different from other nightmares. The simple way she put it was that normal dreams were like looking at a faded drawing of a beach, while the "true" dreams were like actually being there. But why were none of the true dreams good? It was the question Colleen asked most frequently of them.

"Good dreams don't need changing," Ru said.

"It's not fair to show them to me when there's nothing I can do," Colleen replied bitterly. "Not while I'm stuck at Breckenridge."

The rest of the Language Arts class was in higher spirits than they were. The other students were talking about their own experiences in Tanager Park. Ru wondered if her dream would count. Colleen's might, but those dreams never had to do with the park, and Ru kept silent about them at Colleen's request.

Kenna grinned as she approached. After she and Colleen were introduced, she asked, "So have you seen any of the legends yet? I looked out my window at like one in the morning but there wasn't anything in the park."

Ru shook her head. "You can't see the park from my house."

"Oh hey, is that a Carmody necklace?"

Kenna pointed to Colleen's pendant. It was a glassy, inch-long dolphin, a brilliant shade of neon pink. It was far more durable than it looked, too; Ru knew for a fact it had been dropped, stepped on, thrown, and even burned in a fireplace, and it hadn't lost so much as a fin. Ru's mother had guessed it was made of tourmaline, one of Colleen's birthstones, but didn't know if tourmaline could take such abuse and remain as flawless as it was. She also warned that if it was tourmaline, it was worth a lot and could be stolen. Colleen never took it off, not even when she slept.

"No," Colleen said.

Kenna looked for elaboration, but Ru knew she'd get none and stepped in. "Carmody's has only been open for ten years," she said. "Mom said Colleen's mom bought it for her before then."

"I wish I could afford one," Kenna sighed. "Is it true there aren't any two alike?"

"That's what he says." Ru had never seen Ansel Carmody in person, but there were advertisements for his jewelry store at least once a day on TV, and he was listed in all the tourist brochures. "Not many kids have them, even the glass ones are expensive. They're custom-made, you know."

Kenna pouted. "It's not fair. The new girl has *five*. Really!"

Quite a few heads turned in their direction. "New girl?" Ru asked.

"Yeah, there's someone here newer than me," Kenna giggled. "She was in my homeroom. Oh, she's in this class!" Her voice dropped to a whisper. "By the door."

The new girl walked towards Miss Graham's desk, a crumpled class schedule in her outstretched hand. She held herself tightly and avoided looking at her new classmates. It seemed obvious that she didn't want to be there, but it shouldn't have bothered Ru as much as it did. The girl seemed familiar. Very familiar.

"Would you like to introduce yourself?" Miss Graham asked.

With a disgruntled huff, the girl turned on her heels and flashed a huge, almost sarcastic grin. That was when it hit Ru. The girl could easily have been Randy Fresnel's twin. Deep red hair, though kept in better condition, silvery eyes, and a smile that radiated energy and arrogance. She was short, too, though not as short as Randy. The rest of the school year would be trouble if the new girl was anything like him in personality.

"I'm Misty Elesti," she announced. "I just moved to Breckenridge. I came from New Mexico."

Ru blinked, and saw confusion flit across Colleen's face. The fact that this girl supposedly had five Carmody pendants was easily explained; many Breckenridge residents were temporary, sent by wealthy parents who were either away from home constantly or felt their children weren't disciplined enough. But Misty wasn't wearing the uniform, and Colleen hadn't mentioned her. Ru passed a note to

Colleen, who wrote back, *I didn't see her at all yesterday, but they wouldn't let me out of bed very much.*

Misty's gaze swiveled over her classmates with such open disdain that Ru could believe she was from Breckenridge. Then the new girl's eyes settled squarely on Ru. It was so brief Ru shouldn't have noticed. She felt nailed down by that glimpse, and inexplicably vulnerable. She was no longer certain it was Misty's resemblance to Randy that bothered her.

Chapter 6 ★★★ The New Girl

Only one day, and Misty decided that introducing herself as a Breckenridge girl was a mistake. She'd gotten some attention with her Carmody pendants, but few were willing to strike up an actual conversation with her. No one wanted to be friends with a Breckenridge girl. They were confined to the mansion and grounds, except for school and trips the house mothers arranged. Misty had heard houses like Breckenridge used to have their own built-in schools, but for various reasons, Breckenridge sent their residents to public school. She'd heard that part of it was to make sure the girls had some interaction with the outside world, but that didn't work well. There were clusters of matching blue dresses in prime corners of the playground, where the lunch monitors didn't often go. Misty had only seen one of them talk with someone from "the outside" -- the tallest of her housemates, a fragile blonde with perpetually teary eyes.

She'd be stuffed in one of those dresses soon enough. That insufferable Mother Kendrick already suspected Misty of sabotaging the spare uniforms, even though Misty couldn't possibly have known where they were stored or where bleach was kept.

The motion and sound of all the students at play was overwhelming, especially the sound. There were a hundred conversations in earshot, impossible to pick apart. Screaming, laughter, complaints. Basketballs thudded and shoes scraped on asphalt. A garishly-painted football with a four-fin tail gave a whistle as it was hurled skyward. She came to rest on a set of stacked railroad ties that lined the path from the lunchroom to the playground. The leaves of the short, stunted tree she sat under made dancing patches of sunlight and shadows across the ground. The breeze combed her hair, bringing the chill, papery smell of summer's undoing, of old leaves and fire. Winter was as unfamiliar as the tree she sat under, and generally unpleasant from what she had heard.

She hated being here, every minute of it. *He* loved it. He had once told her the best time of year was spring.

Misty gave an exasperated huff as the voice of her "guardian" crept into her mind. She was annoyed with herself for wishing he was there. It wasn't as if she *needed* guidance or discipline, as he insisted. She had enough discipline not to clock him over the head for saying that. It just would have been nice to have someone familiar around. Her stay at Breckenridge, so far from home, was indefinite.

Something crashed into her, nearly knocking her off her seat. Her thoughts scattered, her head flared with pain, her mind boiled with rage. As soon as she regained her balance, she shot to her feet. A boy with startling red hair made a running leap off the end of the railroad ties. "Watch it, moron!" Misty hollered at him.

The boy skidded to a halt and glare at her, fists clenched. Another boy turned as well. She caught a glimpse of his eyes widening before he hid his face entirely behind the bill of his hat. Misty swelled with pride, knowing she was capable of such a withering look, but unfortunately it had no effect on the redhead.

The boy in the hat caught the redhead's shoulder. She heard him whisper, a warning in his words. As good as her hearing was, she only caught that it was a warning, but she recognized the voice and felt a jolt. She had to find out his name. "Who are they?" she demanded of a group of girls nearby.

Two of the girls lowered their eyes to their shoes, but a third said, "The Sox fan is Jayson Hadley. The little guy is Randy Fresnel."

"Who you calling little, Hannah?" Randy snapped at her. "And who are *you* calling a moron?"

Misty stood. "You heard me."

"So you gonna apologize?"

Many of the students had stopped on the pathway to watch them. The basketball had stopped thudding. Jayson mumbled something about not fighting with girls. Misty knew she had to talk to him, but the pain in her head fueled rage too hot to keep inside. "Excuse me? For what? *You* kicked me the head, *you* apologize!"

A fist raised. Misty tensed. She was not used to fighting only with her hands, but her anger urged her to try. It seemed like half the school was gathered around them now. Jayson finally lost his temper, though it was at Randy. "Seriously, stop."

"You heard what she said!" Randy hissed at him.

"I'm starting to think she's right. Let it go!"

Jayson was on her side? That was a surprise. She seized on the distraction and turned to leave. "Maybe you should watch where you're going if you don't want to hear the truth about yourself."

Randy's hand crushed her shoulder. Without hesitation, she grabbed his arm and spun, yanked him towards her, and buried his fist in his stomach. He had started to say something, but the rest of his words came out in a yelp. The crowd gave a collective shout, then fell silent.

Randy didn't fight back. He crumpled and came to rest on his hands and knees. His eyes screwed shut, his mouth gaped, working for air. She looked at Jayson, expecting the next blow to come from him, but he simply backed away, his hands up. She cast her sharpest scowl at the onlookers, and some of them took a step back, too. The Breckenridge girls stared from a distance, their expressions ranging from snide disapproval to fear to delight.

Randy wheezed when she nudged his hand with her toes. "Next time, watch your step," she said.

She walked off just as a lunch monitor dispersed the crowd. Jayson was back beside his friend. She picked up her pace, but all Jayson said to the monitor was, "He got hit in the stomach with a basketball."

"I did not," Randy protested hoarsely.

Jayson cut him off in a voice too low for the monitor to hear, but Misty caught every word. "Shut up! Do you *want* to get suspended?"

Jayson Hadley. She scribbled his name in capital letters as soon as she got ahold of her daily planner. There was more than homework to be done later.

Chapter 7 ★★★ Breckenridge

Breckenridge was a few miles from Quarterhill's main tourist strip, but the Breckenridge girls rarely visited. The house mothers preferred museums and historical landmarks over the gaudy glory of Main Street. Ru's mother used to take Colleen to Main Street every once in a while. Colleen remembered the haunted houses the most, though they never scared her. She admired the props and wondered how much time it took to build them.

Main Street wasn't anything special, Ru said. Just ice cream shops and haunted houses and five different T-shirt stores all selling the same ten designs. Colleen silently argued she'd take an ice cream shop any day over Breckenridge. For once, she thought most of her housemates would agree.

Breckenridge itself was an attraction, though it didn't get as much traffic as Main Street or Tanager Park. It was a historical site with very limited tours. Most people saw the house only from the street. A stark iron-spear fence lined the property, taller than any person Colleen had met. The gate was wide, made of a labyrinth of flat, uneven curls. Mother Fontaine told Colleen it was designed with the leaves of a tree in mind. Colleen thought of it more as the inner workings of a lock.

She wished Mother Fontaine was still there. Most of the girls knew her as Laura; she had been the only house mother who let the girls call her by her first name. She was also the only one who ever tried to talk to Colleen without giving up. Mother Fontaine had bought Colleen her first paint set. The two of them spoke more often in pictures than in words.

Colleen shoved the memory away. Tears threatened when she thought too long of Mother Fontaine. *Proper young ladies hold themselves with dignity*, Mother Kendrick said. *They don't blubber or whine.*

The Breckenridge manor seemed miles away from the bottom of the hill, surrounded by towering oaks and maples. A few willows dragged their branches along the edges of a small pond. The manor was as wide as the high school gym, with lavender walls and navy shutters. Crew cut hedges and rosebushes wreathed the bottom of the house. The porch had a railing like a ribbon of white lace, and a neat row of wicker chairs, all of which stood abandoned at the moment. Neatly abandoned. *Proper young ladies do not leave their chairs facing every which way*, Mother Kendrick said. The rest of the house had the same symmetry to it, as if Mother Kendrick had spoken to it personally.

Mother Grace herded the girls through the gate. She was a tall and narrow woman, whose physical presence was about as scant as her mental one. Colleen could have easily mistaken her for a figure on TV rather than someone actually standing next to her. Under her eyes the girls wandered about the property and lingered on the porch before her plaintive instructions finally nudged them all through the door. Colleen was last. Her feet crunched slowly on the glittering gravel path, her eyes dragged over the ants climbing through the porch boards, on the coral roses bobbling in the breeze. Sunlight grazed the stained glass on the front door and cast a wheel of color on the floor.

Mother Grace disappeared as soon as the group was in the entry hall. Colleen looked everywhere but at the other girls, at the marble floor, velvet furniture, the chandelier with crystals like melting icicles. Most of all, the stairs to the second floor. Until Mother Kendrick came to take roll, Colleen would have to hide, then make her escape to the stairs. Once she reached her room, she would be safe. Mostly.

"Aww, look who made it home. And all by herself, too."

Too late.

Ronnie Kail leaned in the doorway to the south wing, where only the house mothers were allowed. She was careful not to speak loud enough for her voice to carry to the next room. Colleen knew better than to acknowledge her, but there was nowhere else to go. The other girls were watching now, most with scorn, a few with pity.

Ronnie stepped in front of Colleen, her brown curls bouncing. She had a small face with huge eyes that made her look half her age, the perfect front for her snide, sharp tongue. Only Mother Kendrick seemed aware of Ronnie's true nature. "What'd you learn in school today? Numbers, or letters?"

Mutters fluttered in Colleen's ear. It was her own fault, bringing their attention on her with those "nightmares," like they actually happen. Or maybe she really was just scared of the dark. Maybe if she didn't *have* to have a room to herself, she wouldn't be such a crybaby. The whispers of those who believed Colleen's nightmares were worse. *What if she dreams about me? What if she dreams about the house burning down? Don't let her see me.*

"Hi, Colleen!"

She turned, surprised by a new voice. Misty was now in full Breckenridge uniform. She looked strange in it, like she was too tall for it and at the same time too thin. It draped off her like it would on a hanger. "I saw you have a Carmody."

Something shined in Misty's hand. In the many lights of the chandelier, the object seemed to gleam on its own. "I collect them. Maybe we can trade."

The room fell silent. Dozens of eyes locked on Misty.

"It's not a Carmody," Colleen said, voice tremulous. She brushed the tail of the dolphin with her fingertip. "My mother bought it for me when I was a baby."

"You still are a baby," Ronnie said.

That, on top of Misty's frown, sent Colleen scurrying for the nearest corner with tears brimming in her eyes. The only thing that kept the tears from falling was the peculiar expression on Misty's face. Her pale eyes went unfocused, her lips open, as if she was on the verge of speaking, but to no one.

Ronnie put on her sweetest smile and put a hand on Misty's shoulder. Colleen was fairly certain that Ronnie was warning Misty not to make friends. But then, Misty's face froze over. She slapped Ronnie's hand away. Ronnie opened her mouth, but Misty spoke first.

Colleen didn't hear what was said, but all the girls in earshot flinched. Ronnie actually recoiled, wincing, as if she'd been slapped in the face instead of the hand. Colleen had never seen Ronnie afraid. She liked it a lot less than she assumed she would.

Her stomach fluttered with Misty's eyes found her again. Misty had the same calculating expression Ru had when working on a tough math problem. None of it mattered, though. By experience, Ronnie would have Misty seeing straight in a week. Ronnie was in charge of the house mothers, Quarterhill students were ignorant slobs, and the only one worse was Colleen Amundsen. Ronnie had surrounded herself with her friends now. Contempt laced her voice, but her hands trembled. It did seem awfully cold in the hall.

Once the house mothers took attendance, Colleen sprinted for her room. Well, as close as she could to a sprint without being scolded about her manners, which was little more than a stiff, brisk walk. She hurried past the sunburn-pink walls and fluff-filled rooms without looking twice. Her room had not always been on the far end of the north wing, but at a doctor's request, she had been moved. She had a vague, unpleasant memory of the doctor and Mother Fontaine asking questions about her nightmares, and what she remembered about her parents.

The lone room suited Colleen well. She minimized contact with her housemates anyway. Early in the morning, usually before the sun rose, she peered down the hall, looking for lights under the other doors. She went through supper at the very end of the long, lace-covered table with her eyes firmly fixed on her plate. Whether she liked or hated what was served to her, she ate as fast as she could without being upbraided for table manners. At least most of the girls ignored her there. It was hard to get away with anything under the hawk eyes of Mother Kendrick. Colleen didn't like being under her watch any more than being scrutinized by the girls her own age. She was always excused first. Whispers followed her up the stairs. There were no locks on the doors of the bedrooms; when Colleen wasn't the first upstairs, she found things missing. A picture of her parents, one of her diaries. She stopped writing those after she found Ronnie reading the entries aloud to her roommate. The only house mother who didn't act like the theft was Colleen's fault was Mother Fontaine.

For this reason, she kept the dolphin pendant around her neck at all times, even when she slept. Mother Kendrick made her take it off, afraid she'd suffocate in her sleep, but she put it back on after bed check was complete. She could not afford to lose it, especially if it turned out to be made of precious stone. It might be the only thing she had with enough worth to get her away from Quarterhill when she was old enough. Or when she escaped.

One summer night, she would pack all her things in her art supply bag. She would sneak some food away from the dinner table or kitchen, climb that tree on the west side of the property that leaned over the gate, and run as fast as she could before sunrise. Ru could lend her clothes so she wouldn't be running in her easily-recognized uniform. She brought the subject up at school once with Ru, and dropped it after her little brother overheard.

"First of all, Quarterhill's curfew is 11."

"Who says someone'll see her?" Ru shot back. "Besides, she's tall, they might think she's too old for curfew."

Jayson shrugged his sister off. "Second, there's no way you'll get out of Quarterhill before sunrise, even if it is kind of small. You might be able to hide in Tanager Park for a little while, if you don't think the Blue Star is coming to get you," he rolled his eyes, "but I bet that's the first place they'll look for you. Joe Stalvey's dad says that's where they find the most runaways."

The idea had already crumbled in Colleen's head, but Ru wasn't ready to give up. "Did Joe tell you that, or did you hear it from his dad?"

"His dad, when he was here on Career Day. A cop would know, right? Third, no one's going to buy a tourmaline necklace from a kid. They'll either think you stole it, try and find out where you came from and who your parents are, or they'll try to steal it from *you*."

"How do you know?"

Jayson sighed. "Remember that time Randy broke a window on his dad's van?"

Colleen had only met Randy Fresnel a few times, and was happy for so few meetings. He seemed like a compressed spring ("That'd explain why he's so short," Ru said) ready to launch with his mouth or his fists.

Colleen's room was small and her possessions scant. A few carbon copies of her uniform hung in the closet, along with a puffy white parka and her pajamas, freshly cleaned. There was a set of plastic drawers, mostly full of things Ru's mother saved from the Amundsen home before everything was auctioned off. A picture of Colleen's parents and distant relatives, her great-grandfather's engineering textbook with brown pages and a crumbling leather cover, a tiny wooden pot Colleen liked to play with when she was younger, a tape of Colleen's mother playing violin. Ms. Hadley said Colleen's mother had been a songwriter, and the money that was still being made by those songs would pay for Colleen's entire stay at Breckenridge.

The room was different today. The floor had been covered by a plain yellow rug, but Colleen made a mess of it after the dream about Kelly. Her stomach still turned at the memory. At least the smell was gone, though it was replaced by the choking scent of sanitizer. All this she had expected. She was startled to find the other bed in the room occupied.

Three small, worn leather suitcases squashed the frilly comforter on the other bed. One case had its contents spewed across the bedspread, clothes, a pair of frayed, filthy sneakers, and a small makeup kit. The owner of that kit would have to learn to hide it, or it would end up in Mother Kendrick's contraband bin, never to be seen again.

"Oh, so *you're* my roommate?" Misty scoffed. "Good, I thought I'd end up with one of the annoying ones. Your name's Colleen, right?"

Misty resumed emptying her luggage. Colleen's nerves buzzed as she sat down on her own bed. She rummaged through her bookbag, her long hair obscuring everything but the sandy carpet. She heard Misty walk to the closet and back. Metal hangers clanged softly as they were set on the bar.

"Why are the other girls afraid of you?" Misty asked. "Especially that girl, Ronnie."

"Um -- I don't think she's afraid. But I do have bad dreams sometimes. And my birthday's October 31st."

Misty gave a short, confused laugh. "That's *it*? Is 31 an unlucky number or something?"

Colleen stared in disbelief. Was Misty trying to make fun of her? "You don't know about Halloween?"

Misty flung her hands into the air. "I don't know about anything! Do you know how many times the house mothers yelled at me today? Over really petty stuff, too. Especially the old one."

"That's Mother Kendrick," Colleen said. "She's on second watch. She's here until ten every day."

"Does she let you have any fun? Or is that something 'proper young ladies' don't do, as she would say?"

Misty's voice flashed into an impersonation of Mother Kendrick's, near-perfect only ten times more cantankerous. Colleen giggled, despite being nervous that Mother Kendrick could have easily heard. Misty smirked at her. "Really, do you just study when you get home?"

"I like to draw."

Normally Colleen was hesitant about showing her works to the other girls, but Misty actually, genuinely seemed interested. She pulled out her sketchbook. The images within were mostly of outdoor scenery, different angles of the Breckenridge property with the house and birds and flowers she'd seen. Misty's face lit up as she shuffled through the pages. "These are *so* pretty! Could you draw me something, maybe?"

That was a common request, one Colleen usually turned down. "I could, maybe," she said quietly. "But you have to hide it from the other girls. They might rip it up."

Misty's silver eyes widened with shock. She almost seemed offended. "Why would they do that?"

Colleen's voice came out thin through a suddenly tight throat. "Ronnie did, anyway. The other girls just laugh at it. They, um - they tell me my artwork isn't any good. I'm not smart enough to make anything good. Maybe I never will be."

Misty smiled, a bright, warm smile. Colleen wondered why she assumed Misty wasn't capable of such a friendly face. "Oh come on! Don't say things like that. You're the nicest one here I've met so far, and you really do have talent. You should stand up for yourself more."

"You think I'm *nice?*" Colleen said. "Even after I wouldn't trade with you?"

Misty waved her hand dismissively. "I'd be mad if you *did* trade with me and then I found out it wasn't a Carmody, except maybe if yours is made of diamond. But then I'd just feel bad because yours is probably worth a lot more. Hey, want to see my favorite?"

She tucked her fingers into her collar and pulled on a string beneath. It was a gray, silvery cloud pendant with an iridescent sparkle. Though it was easily the prettiest raincloud

Colleen had seen, it was still sad. "A friend of mine back home gave it to me. It's the only one I'd never trade."

"It doesn't look like the other Carmody jewelry I've seen," Colleen said.

Misty's eyes looked beyond Colleen, her cheeks rosy. "It's not."

There was a quiet moment before Misty noticed Colleen's soft, questioning stare. Misty turned nearly as red as her hair. "Uh, anyway! Have you ever tried origami?"

Colleen let her question go unspoken. "Never heard of it."

A binder of colorful paper squares came out of Misty's suitcase. Misty chose a silver leaf, smoothed it out, and went to work on it. She folded, pressed, flipped, pulled hidden prongs from under the paper's umbrella-like folds, until a bird sprang to life out of the sharp corners and points. "It's a crane," Misty said. "You want to learn how to make one?"

A smile cracked Colleen's face. "Sure."

Chapter 8 ★ ★ ★   The Gray Man and the Hawk

A sky, inky, endless, glittering like fresh snow and full of promise. Colleen forgot where she was, forgot that she had been here before. This place was reached by going inward, inevitably the dream took her deeper, and yet she was outside. Inside out, dreaming on the other side of a mirror.

It must have been a great city once. The ground was rusty sand, powder-soft under her bare feet, but cold. She curled her toes and saw the bottoms were stained. Light came from the horizon all around, a ring of molten gold, welding the dome of night sky to the ground. There were what Colleen supposed were ruins, but not ruined, parts pristine and neatly ordered. Whole ivory columns stood like stock alongside stacks of chessboard floors. Heavy stone arches sat on the ground, bridges without roads. Pedestals, elaborate stone railings, in stark black and white. Doors and frames stood on end. Colleen had a feeling if she opened one she might see a gateway into another universe.

Cold wind howled through the ruins, stirring none of the dusty ground, but it came with the first inkling of dread she always felt. Once she recognized the dread, recognized this desolate, sterile desert city, the dread magnified a thousandfold. Her eyes began to dart from place to place, alert for changes. What she was meant to see would come soon, that was assured by memory, but for some reason she felt she could lessen the impact if she could anticipate what was coming. It never worked, nor did trying to force herself awake.

The one comfort she had was that she was always a spectator. She was never involved even if she tried. Once,

two men, giants in her estimation, rolled out from behind a
pillar. Their grizzled faces were taut with rage, yellow teeth
bared. They both had torn leather jackets and jeans smeared
with oil. She could smell their sweat, hear bone and skin
smack when their fists landed. Too real. The bigger of the
two eventually slammed the other against one of the pillars,
stunning him. A switchblade came out. Colleen, knowing that
it was only a dream, felt anger rise within her instead of the
usual fear, and dashed to grab the man's knife arm. She could
see the seams in the jacket's leather, the hair on the back of
the man's grimy hand, real and detailed as anything, but her
fingers went through him as if he was nothing more than
light from a projector.

It would come. Sometimes it came gradually, echoes
of sound from beyond that fiery horizon, coming together
like focusing vision. Sometimes something would
spontaneously fall into the world, like those two men. Colleen
walked, digging her toes in the dust, head swiveling. The stars
winked at her.

To her right there was a path, an opening to a
completely empty plain. A silhouette bobbled in the distance.
Something running. It ran without disturbing the surface, not
a speck of scarlet dust in the air. A human shape revealed
itself. Or was it? A young man, but his skin was gray. Not the
ordinary pale gray of someone badly frightened -- she had
seen enough of that in the bathroom mirror in the morning --
but a dusky, slate gray.

She focused. In her mind, the sterile ruins were
nothing more than one of those haunted houses in
downtown Quarterhill. The young man was a mannequin,
mechanical, predictable. He couldn't hurt her. She studied
him as he came closer. He had broad shoulders, toned arms, a

barrel chest and thin, colorless lips, but also wide hips and curvy legs. His face was soft and round, when his mouth was closed. He reached a hand towards her. It was much flatter than her own, the ends noticeably flared and square. He ran awkwardly, almost tripping over his own feet, as if he wasn't used to running. It might have been funny if he wasn't screaming. There was no sound, but she could see his face clearly now. His eyes were wide, the whites visible all the way around, his face contorted as his mouth worked, flashing flat, canineless teeth. She averted her eyes. The panic in his expression was contagious.

The shadows on the pillars were turning red. The tint of the stars changed. One was shining brighter than the others, right behind the gray man. A bloody haze began to obscure him. Was that star getting brighter? It was, brighter than Mars, almost like the moon, then a distant sun, in thick, bulging crimson.

Colleen imagined the world coming apart. It was a dream, why couldn't it be changed? It was all in her head! She imagined the wind scraping every bit of dust off the ground, breaking what was underneath like thin ice, the columns sucked into the light beyond, the pedestals and floors, the stars bursting like fireworks. Nothing she pictured affected the imagery of the world. Every muscle clenched, quivered, not knowing where to take her.

As she came to the brink of a decision, the bright star flickered and exploded. A monstrous shadow unfurled from the fire, blotting out most of the supernova's light. Vivid red released upon the world, saturating everything from the horizon down to the gray man's dull skin. The shadow stretched, a hawk with clawed wings spread. Colleen's racing heart skipped a few beats. Despite taking up only the moon's portion of the sky, it clouded the whole thing with its cold, jarring presence, its wingspan loomed like an oncoming storm.

The hawk stooped. It came down on the gray man.

The gray man jerked, then his face crumpled in pain. His hands went to his chest a moment before his knees buckled. He dropped heavily into the dirt, revealing the shadow behind him.

The shadow was not a hawk. It was a man, more human than the gray man. Colleen swallowed, her breath short, but she forced herself to look. He was alien too. His proportions were correct for a man, but in the harsh red light something seemed off. His wings had been the ends of his coat, a long, black garment that reached to his ankles. His left eye was covered by his straight, pale hair. The hawkman coldly considered the heap of an alien lying at his feet, then his one visible eye met hers.

Her mind snapped. Everything became impossibly clear, colors burned her eyes, red deeper than the brightest dawn, his eye a colder blue than an arctic sky. Blood smeared the long blade in his hand. The wind gusted, her hair tangled, her skirt flapped, goosebumps spread across her skin. The alien at his feet gurgled and stopped his hoarse, agonized breathing. Sound. *He can't see me*, she thought frantically. *I'm not here! This isn't real!*

He stared. A voice broke through the mist, a shredding sound that not only emanated from the hawkman, but from every part of the cold red world. The stone pillars shuddered, Colleen's brain rattled. Her trembling hands cupped over her open mouth, her stomach lurched. In her darkest nightmares she had never seen, felt, or heard anything so horribly wrong.

He could see her, and from the hard look in his eye, he hated her for it.

The hawkman lunged. Colleen felt herself grow faint. The mist filled her vision with red, then black. She couldn't see, but his footsteps approached. She was not escaping fast enough. This was the end.

A shove, and she found herself staring bleary-eyed at the ceiling of her Breckenridge room.

Shaking violently, she pushed herself up from the carpet. Her blanket draped half on her, half still on her bed. Her head throbbed, probably from hitting the floor. Daylight silhouetted the origami animals that hung in front of the window. The door was open, and Misty's bed was empty. The other girls milled about in the hall.

The hawkman's voice drowned them out. It ran through her head with every throb, though the words made no sense. Confusion threaded through fear. It was a prophetic dream, it had the same feel as the others, but -- aliens? Were the two men wearing costumes? It had to be some kind of show or movie being filmed, she decided. The hawkman's voice hissed in her ear, terror surged afresh. She wrapped the blanket around her shoulders.

The boxes in her closet were overturned and the contents spread across the carpet. The pockets of her coats were inside out. Gritting her teeth, Colleen began to gather the scattered photographs. Who was it this time? Was it worth even thinking about? One last echo of the hawkman's voice in her head convinced her, for now, things weren't so bad at Breckenridge.

Chapter 9 ★ ★ ★ Shawn Lanius

The Ferrari exploded out of the slotted tunnel and whipped sideways, skidded across a road striped with wide arrows, inches away from hurtling through a guardrail and off a cliff. Beyond, the blinding sun blazed over the ocean. The water glinted, hundreds of yellow eyes melting in the incredible heat.

"Hurry up," Jayson said. "We gotta get home."

"Hold on," Randy barked. He threw the wheel to his left and pitched in his seat. He stretched to reach the gas pedal. "One more lap and Randy Fresnel is the winner of the Quarterhill 500!"

There was a squeal and a loud crunch from the game. Jayson groaned and smirked. "You'll have to sew Randy's hand back on before he can hold that trophy."

Randy yelled in frustration, startling a little girl playing Skee-ball behind him. "Vince!"

A broad hand appeared around the corner of the cabinet. "What?"

Randy stormed to the other side, where the opposing driver sat. Vince Faraday leaned casually against the backrest of his seat. His height and build made him look like a junior in high school, rather than the thirteen-year-old he was. "I can't just let you take my high score."

"You only have so many high scores 'cause you cheat!" Randy jabbed a finger in Vince's face. "And you get to play free games!"

Vince brushed his hand away and jumped out of the chair. "You gotta earn that place, short stack. Besides, my name looks nicer up there than yours." He tapped the screen, which was showing the high scores. "See it there? Doesn't it look great?"

"It'd be better without the Packer tribute," Randy growled.

Jayson laughed quietly. Vince was always looking for a reason to mention he was named after Vince Lombardi, for once, Randy had beat him to it. Vince, however, merely grinned.

Though this arcade was on Main Street, right in the middle of the tourist trap, and it was the high season, it was unusually crowded. Even more perplexing, Jayson noticed much of the crowd wore logos from Lakeside University, the community college in Vireo City. Most of them were gathered around an old shooting game with a For Sale sign taped to the corner. The crowd was so thick Jayson couldn't tell who was playing. "What's going on?" he asked Vince.

"New game?" Randy said eagerly.

"No, we're trying to sell that one." Vince looked as perplexed as Jayson felt. He walked to the prize counter. "Hey Dad, what's going on?"

All the kids liked Alan Faraday. The burly, deep-voiced owner of the Alley Arcade was rarely in a bad mood, and gave ticket and food discounts to the locals. A smile curved under his dusty mustache, he looked uncertain, but happy that a few more coins might go into the machines. He had a heavy Wisconsin accent that Vince only echoed in part. "Eh, not sure. I asked around. They said that guy's the lead singer of some band."

"Who?" Vince pressed. "What's his name?"

"Shawn something. He's from Vireo City. I guess the band's getting real popular. I heard they were on Channel 6 the other day."

"Shawn Lanius?" Jayson and Vince exclaimed in unison.

Without waiting for a reply, the two rushed to the fringes of the crowd and tried to push their way through. "Wait, who?" Randy called. Despite not recognizing the name, he pushed as hard as either of them.

"Haven't you ever heard of the Shaddow Puppets?" Vince said.

Randy's expression soured. "Isn't that one of those sissy boy bands?"

"Not even close," Jayson said.

"They played at the big festival last year, remember?" Vince added. "Oh wait, sorry, your parents probably didn't let you stay up late enough to see them."

Randy shook a fist at him. Vince yawned. "Didn't you get beat up by Misty Elesti at recess?"

There was little room around Shawn himself, but Jayson picked him out of the crowd easily. He was on par in age with the crowd, with slick black hair and tan skin. He was taller than Jayson thought, and built in a way that was more imposing than his razor-thin figure should have allowed. He wore neat black jeans and a black collared shirt with a silver image of barbed wire across the chest. Jayson didn't know the game he was playing well enough to tell how he was doing, but Vince was nodding his head approvingly. Eventually the screen went red and the crowd groaned. "Continue?" popped up above a counter.

"You're pretty good at that game," Vince called. "It's for sale, you wanna buy it?"

Shawn barely glanced at him, but gave a lopsided grin as he put the light gun back in its holster. "You must be the owner's son."

If Vince was shocked about being recognized, he didn't show it. He merely gave a confident nod. Shawn answered the question before Jayson could ask. "They warned me about you. I see your name all over these machines. You taking over the arcade when your dad retires?"

Shawn had a slight accent Jayson couldn't recognize. He'd never noticed it when he'd heard Shaddow Puppets' music, and he'd heard their songs often. Ru had bought their CD at the festival. Their mother had gotten it signed once she learned Shawn and Jeremy Shaddow, the band's founder and lead guitar, were being interviewed at her station. It was one of the few bands he and Ru could agree on. Ru liked hard rock, which made up a good portion of Shaddow Puppets' songs, while Jayson normally liked hip-hop and rap.

"If I don't get into the NFL, I'll think about it," Vince said.

"Oh, so you're a football player, too?"

Randy butted in before Vince could reply. "Yeah, but get this. He doesn't even want to play for the *right* team. He's from Green Bay."

Some of the others in the crowd booed playfully. Jayson was not a football fan, but he recognized the logos. He picked out a few Chicago Bears decals amongst them. One of the girls near the back cheered. As usual, Vince was rather alone in this debate, and as usual, he showed no signs of intimidation. "Uh yeah, who was in the Super Bowl last year?" He cupped a hand to his ear. "How'd the Pack do this week? Oh yeah, Favre got those five measly touchdown passes. Just a team record. Guess that can't compare to the Bears getting stomped by Minnesota."

A pair of quarters glinted between Shawn's fingers. He gestured towards NFL Blitz, over by the wall. "C'mon, kid, let's see how good Green Bay is."

"All right!" Vince's eyes lit up. "It's about time I got a real challenge around here."

"Whatdya mean, a *real* challenge?" Randy shouted as Jayson dragged him outside.

The door squeaked shut. Randy pressed his face on the glass to get one more glare in at Vince. "Your mom's going to throw a fit if she finds out you were here," Jayson warned. "You're grounded, remember?"

"Who's gonna tell her, you?" Randy said.

"Mr. Faraday might -"

Jayson cut off as he nearly ran into someone standing at the mouth of the alley, fearful that it might be Mrs. Fresnel looking for her son. Mrs. Fresnel was wide, but not nearly as tall as the stranger in front of him, and Jayson was sure she didn't own a bright red hooded raincoat. The sun was perched behind the stranger's head, casting deep shadows into the void where their face would be.

The stranger suddenly spoke, what Jayson thought was one word.

Skaeya

"Did you say 'stay here'?" Randy asked, backing away. "I don't think so, dude."

The stranger's movements were completely soundless. Their coat didn't rustle, the one step they took towards the boys never shuffled or tapped against the concrete. The hair on the back of Jayson's neck bristled. This was what his mother always warned him about, those vague, dangerous strangers that he was supposed to take care around and never talk to. He wanted to go right back into the arcade, but he was frozen, his feet melded to the sidewalk. He sought the stranger's eyes in the darkness.

He found them and lost all thought. There was no fear left, just an inexplicable sense of awe.

The stranger turned and left.

Jayson's feet came unglued from the concrete. He immediately backed away from Main Street. "Who?" Randy started, stunned. "Who was that? My dad's right, this town is full of weirdos."

A glint caught Jayson's eye. He saw loops of thin silver chains near the foot of the garbage can by the arcade door. He went back and scooped the chains up, drawing out two pendants attached. The pendants glimmered so brightly in the evening haze they looked to have a light of their own. A ruby wolf and an emerald dragonfly.

"What's that?" Randy asked.

"Jewelry. They look like the stuff that comes out of Carmody's store." Jayson held the wolf up by the chain. There was something pleasant about the way the light struck it. "That guy might have been looking for them. We should go get him."

"Forget it!" Randy shuddered. "First of all, I say finders keepers. Second, I'm pretty sure that guy was serial killer or something."

"What, are you scared?" Jayson asked with a smirk.

Randy turned red. "No!" he barked, marching to the mouth of the alley. There was considerable relief in his voice when he said, "He's gone, anyway."

"It is kind of weird he had his hood up like that," Jayson said. "Let's ask Mr. Faraday if he knows who it is."

Mr. Faraday did not know. He seemed concerned, and offered to call their parents for a ride home, which Randy refused immediately and loudly. Mr. Faraday took the pendants and said he'd ask Carmody if they were his — if they were, the owner might be registered. The two boys left the alley in a hurry, more alert than they had ever been. Even so, neither one caught sight of Shawn as they left. His depthless eyes, sharp and icy, remained on the boys until they were out of sight.

Chapter 10 ★ ★ ★ Never Alone

It took Ru a while to understand what was bothering her about the park. She walked along the edge just as the sun was sinking behind the trees, a weak orange that reminded her more of a lone streetlamp than a star. The sky today was pale and hazy, boring in Ru's opinion, and it would stay that way for a while. The trees still had full leaves; only a few were beginning to decay into yellow and red. A long shadow echoed her movements.

As she passed the entrance to the Cardinal Street parking lot, it finally clicked. Two days until October, Quarterhill's busiest month for tourism, and Tanager Park was deserted. There wasn't a single car in the lot. Empty swings hung straight as the poles that held them up. No robins foraging under picnic tables, no locals walking their dogs. Dust blew off the baseball diamonds, chalk lines faded.

It could have been just like this when her father disappeared. No witnesses. He'd never come home from his maintenance job here at the park. He'd known the paths and the woods better than anyone. He was usually the one to recover lost tourists.

Vince Faraday's father had been one of his friends. Ru sometimes pried more information out of him when she visited the arcade. "Your brother looks just like him," Mr. Faraday said, "Except for the eyes. You have his eyes."

"I know," Ru said. "I've seen pictures."

"Did your mother tell you he was studying to be an astronomer?"

Ru shifted and fastened her eyes on the prize counter. "I don't ask Mom about Dad. She cries when she talks about him."

"She misses him," Mr. Faraday said gently. "They knew each other for a long time. People ask too many questions, I think. Do you still get strangers at the door asking about the Blue Star?"

"Not that I know of," Ru said, surprised. "People really did that?"

Mr. Faraday nodded, frowning. "When your father disappeared, the tourism board wanted to use the case to bring in more money. I think Eric would have loved it, but your mother was against it. You almost grew up in another city."

Ru wondered if that old man that lived across the street from the park had a similar story. Maybe someone from his family disappeared one night. He did shout about the tourism board a lot. "Do you think it could have been the Blue Star?" she asked.

Mr. Faraday laughed, then moved to the counter to take a fistful of tickets from a younger boy. "I really don't know what happened to him, Ru. What I do know is that there have been people who have gone into the woods and never come out." A serious light came into his eyes. "Don't ever go there alone, all right?"

Earlier, Ru had gone to the park with Nathan and Kenna. Now she wished they were still around. She shivered, despite the mild breeze. She was just about to move on when a flicker of light caught her eye. She squinted. An afterimage from the sun, probably.

No. There it was again, a spark like a firefly, but blue instead of green. North, not west.

Ru shook her head, blinking rapidly. It was a camera. Someone playing with a flashlight. Despite her mind throwing out all sorts of rational solutions, she soon found herself standing at the edge of the trees, peering in. She could return with Kenna after dinner, but by then whatever had caused the light could be gone. She compromised with her curiosity and conscience, and went down a woodchip path.

The air dampened under the trees, though the leaves across the path were dry. They skittered and crackled in the wind. Ru started at a loud rustle, then noticed a puffy gray tail wind out of sight behind the trunk of an oak. She kept her head up and her ears and eyes open, barely blinking. Little else moved.

Her father had last been seen near the woods, along with Colleen's parents. It had been a strain on the girls' friendship a few years ago. Joe Stalvey said the Amundsens kidnapped Eric Hadley, or possibly killed him. It was "obvious," Joe said, because Colleen's parents had arranged for their daughter to be cared for, but Eric's disappearance had been a complete surprise to Ru's mother. Most people believed Joe in cases like this, with his father being a police officer and all. It had taken Ru a few weeks and a teacher to understand that even if Joe's suspicions were true, none of it was Colleen's fault.

Ru took another step and felt something yank on her foot. Arms wheeling, she tumbled and landed face-down in the mulch. Whatever tripped her still had a hold on her leg, digging through her jeans. She thrashed with a yelp, then rolled over and groped at her ankle.

Her fingers caught under a loop of blue string. Furious, she wrangled the string away from her foot and threw it at the ground. Why was this here? A prank? She followed it with her fingers to where it was buried in the dirt under the woodchips. A few handfuls of soil aside freed the string from the ground.

The string's anchor was a crystalline pendant. It was a deep cobalt blue, in the shape of a soaring eagle. It looked like a Carmody pendant, possibly sapphire, but more likely glass if it was held by a string rather than a chain. Still, even the glass Carmodys were expensive. Some tourist must have dropped it, but how did it get buried far enough to trip her? And with the string sticking up like that? Besides that, it seemed in good shape. Each feather on the wings was in perfect delicate detail, no cracks or chips, and there was hardly any dirt left on it at all. She brushed the last crumbs off its tiny talons and tail.

A head rush nearly knocked her back to the ground. Static flew in front of her eyes. She wanted to lie down, but she staggered to her feet and nearly froze. This wasn't a normal feeling. It had happened before, in that dream with the aliens. Her head swiveled, quick as a bird. Was she dreaming now? She didn't think so.

Her feet moved on their own, light as air. She barely had the mind to pocket the eagle pendant before it slipped out of her fingers.

The woodchip path ended in rounded bricks. Light shined over a hedge fence, which opened into a garden filled to the brim with brightly-colored flowers and small plants, each labeled with tiny bronze plaques on plastic stakes. At last, there was another person. It was a man in a green polo shirt and khakis, the uniform of the parks department. He caught sight of her and smiled, a welcoming smile that was a stark contrast to the energy that had drawn Ru forward.

"Hello," he said, "Here to see the Quarterstone? Just so you know, the garden closes in fifteen minutes."

She nodded and moved on. Despite being one of the most solid pieces of oddity in town, the Quarterstone wasn't very popular and there were relatively few myths attached to it. Supposedly attempts at vandalizing it had failed; blades broke on its surface and paint melted off. That was no mystery, though. Ru had heard of coatings that would be able to protect the stone in such a way, and she didn't know of many stones pocket knives could carve. Still, there were no stones nearby that matched its composition, and the only markings on it were two crossed lines that divided it into quarters. Like Breckenridge, it was more a place for historians than thrill-seekers.

The Quarterstone sat at the end of a hedge tunnel, under a dome formed by a hedge fence and trees. What was exceptional about the stone was its size. The flat, circular stone could easily fit a pair of cars on its ivory surface. It seemed luminescent in the glow of sunset, the lines barely noticeable shadows.

Suddenly there was a flash, seen briefly through the hedge. Definitely blue. The memory of the windsock people lurked somewhere in the back of her head. In haste to find the source of the light, she searched the hedge for a way through, but it had long been sealed from people who would try to get in without going through the garden. The park worker questioned her as she ran out of the garden, but she was barely aware. Right out of the gate, she left the path and wove her way through the forest towards where she had seen the blue flash.

Her crunching footsteps echoed. She stopped. There was a rapid shuffle, behind her. She was not alone, and whatever it was following her did not want to be seen. It was harder to see now that the sun was down, and her eyes went as wide as they could go, searching between the dim trunks of trees.

"YAHH!"

Ru screamed right along with the figure that had jumped out from behind one of the thicker oaks. Then laughter rang out. Ru recognized a head of thorny red hair. "*Randy*!" she screeched.

Jayson was behind him, doubled over. "You should have seen your face," he howled.

"What are you doing here?" Ru demanded.

"Could ask you the same thing." Jayson wiped his eyes. "You aren't supposed to be here by yourself."

"She wasn't alone," a grating voice said. It had come from above.

Chapter 11 ★ ★ ★ Lightning in the Woods

Jayson squinted up at the softly fluttering leaves. Out of the corner of his eye he saw Ru look around wildly. The voice from above had a metallic edge to it, but it was a human voice, another kid, at that. Ru probably forgot that there were a number of voice-altering toys available for cheap in the tourist trap. What made him jump was that the voice next came from behind Randy. It originally was above, and he'd heard no one climb or jump down from the trees.

"Boo."

Randy sprang high enough in the air to get his sleeve caught on a branch. Ru whirled, then wilted in relief. Misty Elesti stood there, her arms crossed and an amused smile just visible in the fading light. "You," Randy snarled.

Misty returned his glare levelly. While Jayson couldn't help but grin, Misty made him uneasy. She had floored his best friend and the toughest kid in school with a single punch, and showed no nervousness in teasing him. Then again, a lot of people didn't take Randy seriously until he knocked a few of their teeth loose.

"What are you doing out here?" he asked. "I doubt Breckenridge let you just leave. Where's your uniform?"

Misty snorted and smoothed the maroon T-shirt she wore. She had one of her Carmody pendants, a silver cloud that gleamed at the slightest touch of light. It was incongruous with her faded, worn jeans and sneakers. "I don't care."

Randy took a deliberate, menacing step towards her. Ru edged closer. "Back off, short stack."

"Who you calling short stack, birdbrain? Ruster?"

Ru ignored him. "You can get kicked out for leaving without permission," she told Misty.

Misty gave an angry laugh. "Good!"

"Whoa!" Randy cried. "Did you guys see that?"

He stared west, deeper into the woods. The trees were little more than a tangle of black lines in the deepening twilight. Jayson tensed, straining his eyes. The others were silent, leaving only the wind to whistle through the trees and rustle the leaves.

Something flickered. It was filtered heavily by the branches, and dim. It wasn't a flashlight, that was all Jayson knew for certain. He gave a shudder as the breeze seemed to turn cold.

Randy was already heading towards the light. He signaled for the rest to follow. Jayson frowned after him. "Your mom's going to kill you. Seriously, it was probably just a camera." He hoped it was just a camera.

"Chicken?" Randy said. "Figures, your sister's a Ruster."

"Shut up," Ru hissed. "What's wrong?"

She had a hand on Misty's shoulder. Misty's face had gone shockingly pale. Jayson thought she might faint. Her voice was wispy. "We need to go back. What if there's something dangerous out there? The four of us can't take on an adult. Or a bear."

"Says who?" Randy said impatiently. "The Quarterstone's that way. If you're scared, go back."

With that, he disappeared into the trees. Misty gaped, her mouth working, then she turned and went towards the garden. The image of strength and confidence that normally backed her was completely gone.

Ru looked between Misty and Randy, her eyes wide, with a strange reflection in them. They had always been a very vivid shade of sky blue, but in the fading light they practically glowed. Finally, she said, "I've got a really bad feeling about this. Neither one of them should be alone, and I don't think any of us should be here. You get Randy and I'll get Misty."

Jayson nodded without hesitation. "I'll meet you guys at the Cardinal Street lot."

He found Randy crouched behind a dead bush, unusually still and silent. Jayson crept up to him and followed his gaze to the other side of a small clearing, full of old stumps. A man sat on the ground with his legs crossed. He had pale hair in a style Jayson had never seen before, partly swept over half his thin, angular face, partly gathered in a short, flaring tail at the back of his neck, and *blue*, of all colors. A silvery blue, or so it looked in the failing light. The man wore a long black overcoat that pooled around him on the ground, the rusty trim of it an uncrumpled, broken ring. "It's just some guy," Randy whispered.

There was an open textbook in the man's hands. Jayson spotted a stack of books nearby on the ground. "He shouldn't read in the dark."

The man looked at them. He was so still Jayson could barely tell he'd moved at all. His one visible eye stood out, pale as his hair. Jayson felt as if the entire world was focusing solely on him. Randy, of course, did not pick up on this. He stepped out from behind the bush. Before he'd taken his second step, the man was halfway across the clearing. There was a silver flickering in his hands and a metallic scrape.

Jayson gasped and scrambled backwards. Randy's nose was inches from the blade of a sword. "Whoa, whoa, wait!" he screamed, backing away, but the blade had already stopped.

Confusion did little to take the hardness out of the man's expression. His voice was deep, clear, and direct, his words oddly accented. "You are too young to be here at this time of day. Go home."

Jayson turned immediately, but Randy piped up. "Hey! You can't boss me around. You're not my mom."

Clenching his teeth, Jayson was about to point out the poor decision of arguing with a swordsman, when a strange vibration went through the air. The words died in his throat as every hair on his body lifted. He glanced at Randy, who had become a human thistle.

"I said *leave!*"

There was a blinding white flash, a booming crackle, a harsh, sustained buzz. Jayson rubbed furiously at his eyes, at the same time backing away from an intense, wavering heat that had suddenly filled the air. When he could finally see, his mind made little sense of what was in front of him.

The man was clearly visible now, due to the light that seemed to be radiating from his hands. No, not light -- lightning. Thin bolts of electricity shimmered through the air, twining around his outstretched fingers.

The two boys tore back through the forest, screaming at the top of their lungs. Jayson forced his way through tight space, not caring if his jacket tore on the branches. They spilled out of the woods and kept running, not even slowing when they sighted Ru and Misty. Randy reached the picnic table they were sitting at and half collapsed on it, wheezing for breath. Jayson sat heavily on the grass nearby. He spared a glance at the woods. No one seemed to be following them.

Ru jumped up. "What happened? What's wrong?"

Instead of answering her, Randy hollered at Jayson. "OK, if all the legends are fake, what was that?"

Jayson coughed and wiped sweat from under the brim of his hat. "There had to be a broken power line."

"What power lines? There aren't any past the Quarterstone. They're not allowed!"

"A storm," Jayson tried.

"The sky's clear!" Randy's finger trained on some violet cirrus clouds twirling off towards the horizon. "Except for that. Yep. *Real* stormy-looking."

"What are you talking about?" Ru asked eagerly.

"There was some guy with *lightning* coming out of his hands!" Randy's voice was shrill.

"That's not what happened," Jayson snapped.

"That's *exactly* what happened!"

"He could have had a Tesla coil or something! He did *not* just have lightning coming out of his hands. Do you know how ridiculous that sounds?"

"Then why did you run, tough guy?"

"Because the guy had a *sword* and I wasn't going to argue with him!"

"A sword?" Ru said, her expression incredulous. "Like the ones they sell at that import store on Main Street? I don't know what you guys saw, but it isn't supposed to storm for another couple weeks."

"Well I ain't going back to find out," Randy said. "Dude was like --"

"Wait, wait," Misty cut in.

Jayson hardly noticed she was there. She'd had her head down on the table before. "How do you know it won't storm for a couple weeks?"

"I know," Ru replied.

"The weather reports don't even go that far," Misty pointed out. "Besides, it's supposed to storm on Thursday."

Why was Misty questioning Ru about the *weather* of all things, when they had just come out of the woods claiming to have seen someone holding lightning? Ru gazed at the sky down Cardinal Street. "The system that's supposed to bring the storms will be pushed south. It'll be sunny and cold here."

"But how do you *know?*"

Ru shrugged. "It's pretty obvious when you look at the weather maps."

"She's usually right," Randy said. "She never misses the weather reports 'cause she's got a crush on the weatherman."

"Shut up! I do *not!*"

"Um, shouldn't we call the police?" Jayson eyed the woods. There was still no more movement from the trees, but he was ready to take off the instant he saw something. "I don't know what that really was, but the guy still had a sword, and I'm pretty sure he was going to attack us if we didn't leave. It's not his property."

"No," Misty and Randy said in unison.

They exchanged glances. Jayson thought he was looking at twin siblings. "Mom's going to flip as it is," Randy admitted. "It's almost dark. She doesn't need to know I was out here too."

"They'll send me back to Breckenridge," Misty said sullenly.

"You'd better sneak back in while you can," Randy said with a malicious grin. "They said on the tour they chain runaways in the basement and feed them mice."

Misty's voice rose with every word. "If that was even remotely true, *why would they tell a tour group?*"

Jayson urged them along the road. There had to be a rational explanation for what he'd seen, but a man with a sword and a temper was by no means unbelievable. A rational explanation did not mean they were safe.

Chapter 12 ★ ★ ★ Time

Colleen had never painted something that wasn't right in front of her, let alone a scene from her prophetic nightmares. The violence in those dreams would send Mother Kendrick into fits if she saw them on paper. Colleen left that part out for this painting, two simple portraits of the dream figures she'd seen. The gray man was decisively not human, that was made apparent in the shape of his body. With the swordsman, however, she could not pinpoint what made him seem so alien. His voice made her certain -- she shuddered as his raspy words cut across her mind for the hundredth time -- but she'd known he was not human before he'd spoken. In any case, she had little practice drawing people, and she wasn't sure if she would be able to portray either accurately.

She considered asking Misty about dreams. Misty sat on her own bed, cruising through her homework. A brilliant student, according to her teachers, but Misty apparently had a problem with authority. The first few days, she'd refused to eat anything. Colleen saw her throw her lunch straight in the trash at school, or try to trade it for non-food items, specifically jewelry and makeup. Eventually Misty started eating so fast she finished dinner before Colleen. No wonder, she must have been starving.

Unlike Colleen, Misty did not leave the table after she was finished. In spite of how uneasy she made the other girls her first day, she grew to fit in well. Ronnie still avoided her, but the other girls were eager to hear her cynical take on everything from school to the universe in general. Colleen listened in from time to time, from a corner and face hidden behind the cover of a thick book. The others were even a little friendly, now that Misty had assured them Colleen was not some kind of living bad luck charm.

"Time is set," she told them. "It goes in a circle forever. The same things happen over and over. A clock is actually a really good way to show time -- not what time it is, but what time *is*. If whatever happens in Colleen's dreams happens in real life, she doesn't cause them, she just sees them. Get it?"

While Colleen got it, something about Misty's explanation nagged at her. She glanced up. Misty barely looked at the problems in the book before she wrote the answers. "How do you know that time is set?"

Misty returned a quick, somewhat bored glance. "We don't have free will."

Colleen frowned. She felt hesitant challenging what might be her only friend in the house. It was true the others weren't as cold to her as they used to be, but in no sense could she call them friends. "But *how* do you know?" she said softly.

Misty didn't even look up this time. "You just have to think about the way things are. Our choices are made by the way we were born or the way we are raised, right? Either by your genetics or by your environment. Whatever you're born with or taught determines how you'll react to every future situation. It's all one big chain reaction that makes up the whole of time." She caught Colleen's blank stare and set down her pencil. "Why do you always leave the dinner table early?"

Colleen was caught offguard by the question, but saw no reason not to answer with the truth. "To protect my things. The other girls stole things from me when they left the table before me."

"Why do you want to protect your things?"

"Because a lot of them came from my parents."

"Why does that mean anything to you?"

Colleen's voice caught and her lips trembled. Misty immediately unlatched her gaze. "Sorry, I didn't mean to be rude. But the point is, there's always a reason, isn't there? Even if you don't know what it is." She went back to her homework. "I think the real question is, can we ever change it?"

The direction of conversation made Colleen nervous, and not just because the more religious of the house mothers might get worked up over it. Beyond Misty's cynicism there seemed to be something deeper, something more akin to anger and pain, and the simple changes in Misty's expression and voice made Colleen feel like she was getting closer and closer to the edge of a cliff. Thankfully, Misty changed the subject. "I want to know where more of the others come from. It'd be nice to know I'm not the only one being punished."

"Your parents are alive?" Colleen asked sadly. "Are you going home in the summer?"

"Not if they have anything to say about it." Misty grunted. "It's not like I had much to leave behind though. You're the first friend I've had in a while."

Colleen was not sure she believed that, but she felt her heart warm.

"You have friends on the outside, right?" Misty asked. "I see you hanging around with Prudence Hadley a lot."

Colleen nodded. "Don't call her Prudence, though, she hates it. She's been my best friend forever. Our parents were friends too."

"Your parents died?" Misty's voice softened.

Colleen's throat constricted again as a cloud of bad memories unearthed. "No, they're missing. So is Ru's dad. They disappeared the same night, and the last place anyone saw them was Tanager Park."

Misty looked on with suspicion. Rightfully so, as there was a lot Colleen was holding back. She didn't pry, though. "My parents think I'm a monster. Not in a cute way like some people call Ronnie. They actually think I'm possessed by a demon or something." She gave half a smile. "I guess it isn't all that shocking. They thought everything was demonic. Hey, can I see what you're working on?"

Colleen gingerly propped up the painting. There was a silence.

"What is this?"

"It's from a dream I had. What's wrong?"

Misty stared at the painting oddly. She almost looked alarmed. "They're kind of familiar," she said at last. "Maybe I saw them in a dream too. Wouldn't that be weird?"

"It really would."

Chapter 13 ★★★ Meeting

There were too many crowds in the park in October, too many ghost hunters and students and festivals. Even in the dead of night Kestrel was bound to run into someone with a camera. He'd grown a little too efficient at breaking them. No one felt the matter was worth pursuing once they found themselves at the sharp end of his blade, even those impaired by sleeplessness or alcohol, but he was starting to become a legend himself.

In truth, part of the blame rested on him. He visited the park far more often than he should. Tanager Park had a haunting beauty to it in the fall. These were the days a thin mist erased the bottoms of the trees in the shallow valley. Chilled breezes blew clouds of burning foliage from the shivering branches, leaving crows and hawks with nowhere to hide. The fading grass glistened with dew and silvery spider webs, and the lakes were placid even with geese crowding their shores. The world was settling in before a big sleep, the first bright flickers of dreams to come.

Nighttime was less impressive. Quarterhill was too close to Chicago to see the open stars. Some of Kestrel's acquaintances actually preferred the city, Shryke, for one. It was nearly four in the morning when Shryke appeared at the edge of the park. He leaned against a sign under a trail map shelter, his hands resting in his pockets and his dark eyes dreaming. The air around him reeked of stale smoke. He was ruffled, his inky hair mussed, silk shirt wrinkled. His feet were invisible under the river of fog that had crested the valley and now flooded Cardinal Street. "How's it going?" he said in a slightly hoarse voice.

Kestrel's words cracked with a warning. "You're late."

"Relax." Shryke gave a half-smile to offset the shudder than rippled through him. "The sun isn't up for another couple hours."

"Where were you?"

"Show ran long, then the freeway was clogged." Shryke looked away, but clearly felt Kestrel's level, bullet-like stare. "Dude, what was I supposed to do? I was in a van with the rest of the band. I can't just zap away from them."

At last, Kestrel answered, "You are not a resident here. Remember that."

Shryke's voice raised. "Do you understand the complexities of this society at all?"

"These people *work* to believe the deception that rules their lives every day, and you mean to tell me you cannot play to it?" Kestrel interrupted. "There will always be someone to offer a rational explanation if you cannot. Did you see the Skaeya?"

"Yeah. Find something new?"

"Sylph's initial report indicated they are only children."

Shryke snorted. "They are. I saw two of them at an arcade downtown. It's supposed to be an insult, right? That's what I take it as."

Kestrel turned away, his long hair concealing his face from Shryke. He waded through the fog, boots soundless on the gritty concrete. A few seconds later he heard Shryke's clumsier, scratching footsteps as he hurried to catch up. "They would never take such measures merely to insult us. It is either desperation or a distraction."

"But seriously, they were ten years old." Shryke arched an eyebrow. "I didn't notice anything special about the two I saw. There would have to be something incredible about them to be a distraction. How many of us are there? A million?"

"Fifty seven billion, three hundred thousand and eighty-four," Kestrel corrected automatically. It was one of his jobs to know, down to the very last one.

"Yeesh."

"You have a point. It would be ludicrous to try and lure us with such small bait. Nevertheless, in case this is a trap, I want you to assist Sylph in this matter."

"How?"

"Bring them to me."

Shryke looked both concerned and annoyed. "What for? They ain't any good to us."

"If we can convince them to support our cause, we will spring no traps. We can at the very least force them to give up their talismans. However," Kestrel looked Shryke dead in the eye, "It is absolutely essential that the children are brought to me before they are informed of their true nature. Afterwards our choices are severely limited."

"Or we could just kill them."

Kestrel glared. Shryke shrugged and rolled his eyes. "Fine."

He quickened his pace and veered off towards a side street. Kestrel watched impassively. "Shryke."

Shryke sighed and turned around.

"You are to return to base and accompany Karacara until Sylph is prepared."

"What? No!"

"She specifically requested you." Anyone but Kestrel would have sounded smug.

"That doesn't mean you have to say yes!"

Shryke waited with his arms flung wide open, as if he expected Kestrel to admit to a joke. "Find a better way to escape your entourage next time," Kestrel told him.

Muttering and no doubt cursing Kestrel under his breath, Shryke snapped his fingers. False light flowed from the ground in spiraling tendrils, turning the serene blue of the street a sickly yellow. Shryke vanished along with the light.

A thought hitched in Kestrel's mind. The sleeping neighborhood was bathed in pure azure, yet the streetlights here were orange. His hands crept under his coat and gripped his sword handles before it occurred to him that weapons would be useless. His voice split the silence, calm and clear. "These woods are a bit shallow for you to be here, aren't they?"

The fog burned away under the Star as it drifted into sight, its own glittering mist trailing behind. The white fire at the Star's core was blinding. Kestrel released the swords, but his mind was armed. "Clearly our meeting was not coincidental. What is it you seek, Caere?"

A loud rumble answered him. Kestrel dived for the ground. Before he landed, the Star unleashed a massive beam of solid blue-light white. The heat of it seared through his overcoat. His eyes watered and vision blurred as the force of the beam rattled his skull. He caught the trembling concrete with one hand and rolled nimbly into a crouch. On one knee, he pressed his hand harder into the ground and closed his eyes. He had decades of practice, but the energy the Star was releasing forced him to use all the focus he could muster. The electricity resisted his commands, threatened to shred him as it poured into his arm, shook his bones as it protested being confined. Sparks glimmered over his fingertips. He waited for what seemed like an eternity, with only a fierce determination keeping his body and mind from being ground away by the raging forces around him.

The beam vanished, leaving a dazzling afterimage. This would be the Star's weakest point. He sprang up and jabbed his hand towards the Star. Lightning exploded from his fingers, deafening thunder ripped through the still air and echoed for miles. As the electrical barrage hit, the star wavered and scattered like a reflection on a pond. His throat clenched as it quickly began to reassemble.

Was this part of a trap? Kestrel was always at a disadvantage here, but the Star normally didn't go on the offensive. He sensed there was indeed a sort of desperation behind this attack. He was tempted to stay and find out more, but he wasn't sure he would survive a direct hit.

The others had to be warned. Kestrel resigned the battle in a whorl of negative light.

By lunchtime, Randy's story about the man with lightning in his hands was all over school. Ru guessed he found telling the story worth being grounded further over. Misty wasn't as angry as Ru expected, but she was still sullen about returning to Breckenridge. She was also strangely meek, as if she'd been caught. Colleen said that no one had noticed Misty's absence. Not even Colleen had known her own roommate was missing. "I thought she was with the other girls," she said.

"The other girls thought I was with you," Misty told her.

Misty was starting to replace Nathan in Ru and Colleen's group. It wasn't as if Nathan minded. He and Kenna were rarely seen apart these days. But Ru found Misty to be somewhat uneasy company; her cynicism rivaled Jayson's, and there was still something about her Ru couldn't put her finger on. For Colleen's sake, though, Ru was welcoming.

Unfortunately, Ru was often left alone to explore the park, as Breckenridge girls had to return home straight after school. She'd had second thoughts about not going with Jayson and Randy the instant she'd turned to follow Misty out of the woods. It could have been a prank, and Jayson shrugged it off as some kind of publicity stunt, but once a teacher took Jayson aside and confirmed what he had seen, Ru really started to believe. Jayson denied most of what Randy said, but he was insistent he'd seen a man with a sword. That was of enough interest to draw a crowd around him while he walked down the halls. Suddenly everyone was making plans to go to the park after school, but no one Ru really knew.

It wasn't fair that she never got to see anything weird like that. She was the one that was looking for it. Jayson didn't believe in it at all.

She opted to walk home, to spend an hour or two in the park. She'd settle on a picnic bench or swing and wait to see if anyone familiar showed up. It was unlikely. She didn't have a significant number of friends like her brother.

The sky today, as she'd predicted, was a cloudless and hazy bland blue. She walked to the edge of the street and shaded her eyes against the sun. Figures of Tanager Park legend rarely made an appearance in the daylight, and there were many people still around. The baseball diamonds were full. Tourists lugged carts full of camera equipment, coolers, and layers of clothes along the pathways. And then there was --

"Hey!"

Ru's first instinct was to ignore the man. There he was again, leaning over the rail of his porch as she had seen him so many times before. She was surprised she hadn't heard his usual tirade halfway down Cardinal Street.

"Hey kid, wait! You, little girl in the yellow shirt!"

Startled, Ru pointed to herself. The man nodded and motioned for her to come closer. Ru was halfway up his driveway before she remembered she had no idea who he was, and he seemed like an especially volatile stranger at that. "Come here," he ordered.

Ru didn't budge. She spared a glance behind her. Good, there were other people within earshot. "No. What do you want?"

The man didn't press her. His deep scowl seemed normal, but there was sadness in his eyes. "Oh no," he murmured, shaking his head. "Listen to me. If someone asks you to follow them into the woods, don't do it."

"OK," Ru replied. "Everyone says that."

"If I were you," he continued, in a soft voice unlike anything she'd ever heard from him, "I'd take that necklace back to the woods and bury it. Leave it. Never look back."

Her mouth dropped open and her fingers flew to the eagle pendant, which hung openly around her neck. No one had said anything about it yet, nor had there been any advertisements for it. Even her own mother had overlooked it. "How -- how did you know I found this in the woods? Is it yours?"

"No, it's yours," he said reluctantly.

"Oh no," Ru held the pendant out to him. "I can't –"

"NO!" he shrieked. He flattened himself against the front door, his wrinkled hands scrabbling for the knob. "Keep it away from me! Get rid of it, I said!"

Ru bolted away.

She sprinted until the park was no longer in sight and she felt like her lungs would burst. She stopped at a corner some distance from the park to catch her breath. The pendant was cold in her hand, smooth and shining. She'd never heard a grown man scream like that, and hoped she never would again. He wanted her to throw it away, but then said it was hers? It made no sense. Part of her was scared into thinking that ridding herself of the pendant was a good idea. But in truth, she felt like the pendant was right where it belonged.

Chapter 14 ★★★ Gatestone

The Hadley house seemed much busier than it should have been with only three people in it, mostly due to Ru's mother. Ms. Hadley always left an article she needed buried in a pile or her press badges in odd places, not easily remembered. Pizza was the order of the night, which Ru and Jayson never objected to. Ms. Hadley pinned a slice between her own teeth as she went for her shoes.

Ru chewed absentmindedly, rummaging through a book she'd checked out from the library. It was the oldest book she could find on the history of Quarterhill, from the school library, not very old. Jayson leered across the table at it. "It's rude to read at dinner, you know."

"Don't the teachers ever yell at you when you don't take your hat off inside?" Ru retorted.

"Whatcha reading?"

"It's a secret."

"OK," Jayson replied through a mouthful. "Hey, want some seafood?"

"Jayson, don't do that," Ms. Hadley groaned.

"Hey Mom?" Ru turned away from her book, just in time to catch her mother before she scuttled off to another room. "Who is that guy up on Main Street who's always yelling at everyone?"

Ms. Hadley rushed out without answering, then returned with a folder and set it on the counter next to the empty pizza pan. "Older man? Blond, lives across from the park on Cardinal Street?"

"Yeah! It's a tan house with a big porch."

Ms. Hadley frowned. "Why do you want to know about him?"

Ru was taken aback by her mother's alarmed expression. She didn't especially want to give away she'd been talking to a stranger. Her mind worked quickly. "My friend Kenna lives by him and she's kind of scared of him."

"He's just angry about town politics, hon. He wouldn't hurt your friend." Ms. Hadley sounded like she was trying to convince herself. "He's a veteran, so try and show him a little respect, OK? Jan's going to be over in a little bit. I'll see you in the morning. Love you."

"Bye, Mom," Ru and Jayson answered in unison.

Jan had been their sitter before Kelly, before getting a full-time job at a factory. Ru was looking forward to seeing her again. Jan told Ru as many useful things about Mr. Hadley as Mr. Faraday did.

"What's Mom doing today?" Ru asked after the garage door had hummed shut.

"Breaking news," Jayson said. "Something about the President."

Ru let her pizza slice sink to her plate. "I wish she could stay for dinner more."

Jayson shook his head. "Yeah, but then we wouldn't be eating pizza. It's be like brussels sprouts or something."

"Mom hates brussels sprouts. She wouldn't make us eat them."

"She'd make us eat *some* vegetable." Jayson picked up his last piece. "Why'd you ask about that guy?"

"He said something weird to me today. Remember this?" She touched the eagle pendant. "It might be his."

"Really?" Jayson was quiet for a moment, then asked, "You ever seen him in a red coat?"

Ru's mind prickled. "Why do you ask?"

The front door creaked open.

Their eyes darted towards the door, then to each other. Ru got up and stopped before she even left the kitchen. The door was open wide, the cool evening air pouring in around a woman on the front porch. With the porch light off, Ru couldn't see much about her. The woman had long hair in a high ponytail, and a long coat that waved oddly in the wind, as if it was made of something stiffer than cloth.

"Hey, you're not Jan," Ru said sharply. "Go away!

The woman held out a hand. "You forgot these."

Jayson started towards the door, but Ru blocked him with an arm. The stranger turned her hand over, revealing sparkling red and green crystals. "Oh!" Jayson said. "They're not mine -- wait, how do you know I turned that in?"

The woman took a step forward and opened her mouth to speak.

Her voice was engulfed by blue light that suddenly burst from her chest. Her body was swallowed in a silent flash. Ru yelped and nearly knocked Jayson over as she jumped back. The wind pushed the door open again.

"One *is* yours, of that you are well aware," the Blue Star said. Light wisped off its surface like thick steam.

The crystals lay on the floor. Pendants, just like the one Ru had around her neck. Jayson, without a trace of fear, approached them. He picked up the red crystal. A wolf's head. As soon as he straightened, a thin beam shot out from the core of the Star and grazed it, as well as Ru's pendant. She stood frozen, but felt nothing, as if the beam was simply light. When the beam vanished, Jayson's pendant had changed. It was a round symbol, a silver four-point star surrounded by four white, feathered wings, supported by a gold hoop and held together in the center by a red gem. She lifted her own pendant and saw the same symbol, only with a blue gem.

"Follow me," the Star said.

"Why?" Jayson demanded.

"You are in danger." The Star's voice was calm but stern. "You will gain nothing by hiding here. Your door was locked when I arrived."

There was no doubt in Ru's mind, for once. Jayson, however, stood where he was, his eyes shadowed by his hat. At last, he smiled. "Well, since we're dreaming, we might as well go."

Ru knew the Star was anxious. She did not know how. It was the same feeling when she understood it was looking at her, even though it had no face. Was that woman still in there somewhere, just behind the light, or had the woman just been a disguise for the Star? It floated down the driveway and Ru walked after it. She heard Jayson close the front door before he caught up.

Her head was fuzzy, warm, her feet light. There was no sound. Ru realized just how much she could usually hear at night, cars, crickets, dogs barking. There was complete silence now. What more, all light was blue. The streetlights were a dull navy, porch lights dim and icy, shining on the street like moonlight on snow. Even the stars, peering out from the gaps in the thin clouds, were all tinged with blue. All wind had died. It had to be a dream, like Jayson said, but despite her clouded head she was aware. It felt real. Every leaf resting in the grass was clear to her, every brick and tile of the houses they passed. She pinched her own arm with her short, uneven nails. The pain was sharp, but the world did not change.

The Star approached a tall gate. Ru vaguely recognized it as the gate in front of Breckenridge. Colleen waited behind the gnarled iron vines. Her ever-present dolphin pendant was no more, replaced with the same winged symbol Ru and Jayson had received. The gem gave off a glow that illuminated her face just a bit.

"Colleen, what are you doing out here?" Ru asked in a low tone. "Won't you get in trouble?"

Colleen's voice seemed to be coming from a more distant person. "I had a dream. It's all happening here. Even my pendant turned into -- this." She sounded sad but accepting.

"When?"

"I fell asleep after I got to my room today. All we need now is --" she raised her head. "--a little boy with red hair."

"OK, look. I'm not *little*."

Randy sauntered up to the group. "The other pendant belongs to him," the Star told Jayson.

Ru's face fell. "You had to bring *him*?" she grumbled at the Star.

The Star smiled an invisible smile. "It was not my choice."

Randy took the dragonfly pendant with some hesitation. When the Star changed it, it blazed with neon green light. Randy looped it around his neck without questions.

"We must go to the Quarterstone."

"But the gate's locked," Colleen said.

She jumped as the bulky lock at her hand gave a piercing *plink*, and the gate groaned as it inched open. She took a small step outside, biting her lip, looking all around, and rushed to Ru's side. As if Ru could do anything to stop the Breckenridge house mothers, should they see Colleen leave, or the Star if it had ill intent.

The Star lead them through the botanical gardens, through the tunnel that went to the back of the visitors' center. Even the forest was silent, no tourists, no owls. The children huddled together as they walked towards the Quarterstone. A gentle ivory light shone from the end of the hedge tunnel, just barely visible beyond the fires of the Star. It was the stone itself. It was radiating enough just enough light to touch the tops of the trees. Sort of like an Aurora Pool, Ru thought, it looked like a lake of light on the ground.

"What you know as the Quarterstone," the Star said, "is known elsewhere as a gatestone. You are the only ones in the city who can use it. Stand on it."

All but Randy hesitated. He shot the others an annoyed look. "Isn't this the part where people disappear?" Colleen asked.

"Who cares?" Randy laughed. "The legends say the Star sounds like a monster. Obviously that isn't true."

"We have little time," the Star urged.

"Come on," Randy said. "Even if no one ever hears from us again, we'll be the only people in town that know the truth."

"If we're not disintegrated," Jayson said in a disturbingly calm voice.

Randy gestured towards the Star. "We already know the Star exists now. You can't tell me you don't want to know more."

"It's a dream," Jayson said flatly.

Ru rounded on him. "If you're so sure it's a dream, why are you worried about being disintegrated?"

Jayson opened his mouth, but Colleen spoke first. "It's not a dream. I know what a dream feels like from the inside. Whatever happens to us here is real. That's why we should be careful."

The Star shifted. Ru didn't like it. It seemed to be scanning the trees, and though any nervousness she had was numbed by the pendant, her imagination was in full form. Anything could be in that dark forest beyond. She stepped up on the stone. Jayson eyed her placidly, then did the same. Colleen was the last, cringing as she placed her second foot on the stone. Stepping on the stone had not been forbidden by park authorities, but Ru recalled a legend or two mentioning it was bad luck, along with some dubious examples to go along. A man's car was stolen from the parking lot after he'd walked over it. A child playing on it tripped and broke an arm. Ru's mother said to stay off of it, and her first step felt like she was climbing up on the kitchen table.

The instant Colleen's foot touched down, wind gushed in from all directions. The trees whipped into a fury, leaves fluttered and spun around them as the stone's glow intensified. Ru cried out as fire burst up from the edges of the stone, a high, flowing circle of glistening flame that seemed to be all colors at once. Pressure built, the wind changed direction, coming from beneath them instead of swirling around them. Ru felt lighter than ever, almost as if her shoes were lifting off the stone. A white beam of light shot into the sky.

All the noise, light, and wind died away. Ru was facing the outside of the stone now, her back to her friends. She was suspended in the air a few inches above it somehow, everything frozen. Then the suspension broke, and they stumbled away from each other. The Star was gone.

The first thing Ru did was look up, and her breath caught when her eyes found the sky. Even blocked by a cover of long, broad leaves, the sky sparkled with an intensity she had never seen before, even in her dreams. The air was thicker and warm, and carried the scents of salt water and strange flowers.

"What happened?" Colleen gasped. "Ru?"

"Wait a minute." Randy was looking to the sky too. "Where are we? The park?"

They all inched forward, squinting at the foliage beyond the stone. The ground was sandy and soft, dazzling in the intense starlight. There was a small clearing nearby, surrounded by short, leafy bushes and trees with slim, limber trunks. A path ran off into the woods, and beyond there were small yellow lights like frozen fireflies.

"These look like palm trees. Sort of." Ru scrutinized the leaves above. "Quarterhill is too far north for those."

"This is the only continent of the planet Iresca."

A light flared up behind Jayson. As Ru's eyes adjusted to the sudden brightness, she made out a large hummingbird in the center of the light, perched on top of a bush. It had a long, flowing, curled tail and tiny black feet, and prismatic feathers that gave off a sharp glittering glow. It watched them out of one white eye.

Jayson turned slowly, trying not to scare it. "I think this bird just said something."

"Parrots talk," Ru pointed out. "I don't see why other birds can't."

Jayson lifted the bill of his hat and leaned towards the bird. Its head twitched upward to meet his eyes. "Parrots don't glow," he concluded.

"Neither do glass necklaces," Randy said.

"I'm a lytra."

The voice clearly came from the bird. It sprung into the air, its wings becoming a blur. The higher it flew, the brighter its feathers glowed, until it dissolved into a light like the Star. Ru shielded her eyes.

"You may call me Fuse," it said. It had an accent that mostly affected its vowels, but there was something familiar about the way it spoke. "I see I disturb you as I am. This may help."

The bird flashed, and the light fell away in sparks. Glowing feathers littered the ground. In the bird's place stood a tall, charcoal-skinned human. Ru had never seen a person like this before, slender but sturdy, rainbow eyes, squarish fingers. Colleen gave a small whimper, and Ru noticed she was wide-eyed and paler than ever. So much for not being disturbing.

"I first ask that you listen to my story," Fuse said, "And what will be yours. No one will notice you have left your homes."

"That's supposed to make us feel better?" Jayson scoffed.

"As I said, you are no longer on Earth, but the planet Iresca. It orbits a star on the opposite side of the galaxy, which you call the Milky Way. We know it as Kelsilde." She swept her hand in an arc over her head, tracing the stars. "Kelsilde is part of a system of twenty galaxies."

"Isn't that the Local Group?" Jayson said.

"The Accilean System," Fuse corrected. "I represent this galaxy in a council that is dedicated to protecting the system and guiding its people to live their best lives. You have been called here because we need you."

Somehow, she looked all four of them dead in the eye at the same time. "Your planet, which we call Skae, is outside the system. It is the one sleeping planet within the twenty galaxies. Because you are outside the system, you are the only ones who can help us. You have been chosen to be Skaeya-cyu – 'flying fighters,' as you would say. Warriors who protect the System from invaders. Through the System, you can harness power to aid you, power you never thought possible on your planet. It is not an easy task, but you will not be alone."

The four responded with a silent stare.

"This is a pretty good prank," Randy snickered. "How'd you do the special effects? I bet Joe could never come up with something like this."

Prank, dream, the words did not fit right in Ru's head. They were obviously in a completely different place, and she trusted Colleen's judgement about dreams. "We're just kids," she said at last. "How can we defend galaxies?"

Jayson was already wandering off. "No thanks," he said, "I don't really want to dream about being a superhero."

"Wait!"

Fuse's voice rose in a frightening way, and startled Jayson into looking at her again. Ru saw tears brimming at the edges of her eyes. "Please, don't go. I know it is a lot to ask of Skaeyans your age, but we truly do need you."

Colleen, surprisingly, was the first one to speak up. "It isn't a dream. We should listen."

Jayson crossed his arms. "OK, let's say we're not dreaming somehow. Ru brings up a good point. Why kids? Why not Secret Service agents or the Army or police? Why not *you?*"

Fuse quickly regained her composure. "Members of the Accilean Council are not allowed to fight. I cannot answer for the others. I do not choose the Skaeya."

Jayson's scowl deepened.

"You don't seem to realize how serious this is," Fuse said. "If you refuse to become our guardians, then you, everyone on your planet, everyone in this galaxy, will certainly die."

Chapter 15 ★ ★ ★ Switch Meteor

Silence fell across the clearing. "Why?" Colleen whispered.

"Because of the Lraenu."

Ru flinched. "Lraenu" felt like it could break her ears if Fuse had said it louder. Though she was hesitant to ask what a Lraenu was, she did. She could not pronounce it the same way Fuse did.

"The first of our Skaeya rebelled against the Accilean Council," Fuse said. "Since then, the galaxies have been under attack by his soldiers -- vicious, ghostly creatures we call Lraenu. The Lraenu can shapeshift, but in their true form they are practically invincible. Practically. You four have the power to stop them."

"Cool," Randy said.

"But we don't have power," Ru said.

"You will soon. Not long ago, one of our agents contacted you. You did not know what was happening at the time, but he was taking the material necessary to make those talismans you wear. He activated your power and it has been building since then." Fuse knelt in front of Ru. "What is your name?"

"Ru."

Fuse pointed at Ru's pendant. "These talismans have been granted to help you access your tools. It is important that you always keep the talisman with you. Consider it a part of you. Don't lose it. Don't give it up. Most importantly, don't break it. Ru, I can sense it will be easiest for you to learn how your power works. First, you must arm yourself." Fuse rose and backed up a few paces. "Call out, 'switch meteor!' as loud as you possibly can. As if you wanted the sky itself to hear you."

Ru looked at the others, searching for a hint of what to do. All eyes were on her, Jayson skeptical, Colleen nervous, Randy intrigued. It couldn't hurt to say a few words, she reasoned. The forest was too quiet to be screaming, but Ru sucked in a slow, deep breath. "*SWITCH METEOR!*"

The cry echoed through the trees. After a few seconds of silence, she was sure her face was a bright enough red to see in the starlight alone. The fact that none of the others were laughing kept her calm. She expected Randy to be cackling, but he looked disappointed instead. "What's supposed to happen?" Ru asked Fuse. "Why'd you make me yell like that?"

Colleen gasped. "A shooting star!"

At first, Ru could only see the twinkle of strange constellations. Then, a glittering blue streak of light came into view. "That's too big to be a shooting star," Jayson said. "And too slow."

A breeze kicked up. The palms swayed, hissing ominously, and suddenly the stirring of air felt more like a storm was moving in. The star ballooned to the size of the moon and lost its tail. "I think it's heading this way," Randy gulped. "Run!"

The entire forest turned blue-white under the light of the incoming meteor. The trees thrashed as the wind gusted in. The winds pushed everyone away from Ru. She stood motionless at the center of the storm, unable to take her eyes away from the sky. Randy and Colleen locked their arms around tree trunks to keep from being blown away. Jayson had dropped to the sand and was clawing his way back to his sister. "Ru! Ru, move!"

His voice was so distant. Her ears were filled with the rush of air. The light of the meteor blocked everything out.

It hit. The impact knocked her spirit from her body. She was rising upwards at an incredible speed, through clouds, through the sky, stars and suns swirling endless all around her, all reaching for her. When they touched her, something inside shattered.

She never felt so free.

Abruptly she was back in the forest. She was keenly aware of every one of those trees, every grain of sand under her feet, all the stars overhead, even what she couldn't see. Her nerves hummed with the energy of it all. The absolute clarity of her mind and senses astonished her. Fuse was close by now, and even without light, she somehow radiated color even more vividly than when she had been a bird.

Colleen peered out from behind her tree. "You're -- you're different."

Ru glanced down. Her clothes had changed, though they didn't look all that out of the ordinary. A blue t-shirt with white sleeves, black jeans, blue sneakers with white wing decals on the side. A blue headband with long tails was tied firmly around her head, and there was a barrette above her right ear that she couldn't see. A tiny light pulsed inside the gem of her pendant, something she would not have noticed if her senses hadn't been heightened.

At the same time, Colleen and the others were different as well. It was as if Ru had stepped into a movie and they were figures in the oldest, grainiest black and white photo. They were lifeless, missing details. They approached slowly, wide-eyed.

"You are the Skaeya of the Sky," Fuse told her. "The leader of this generation."

The weight of the word "Skaeya" hit her opened mind with full force. In that instant she knew just what a Skaeya meant to the galaxies, what was waiting inside her to be awakened. She felt like a star just lit, burning with unimaginable energy.

"Hey, can I do that?" Randy asked eagerly.

Fuse smiled more openly now. "Give it a try."

Randy's meteor didn't take nearly as long to arrive as Ru's. It fell so fast Ru barely saw it land. The light it created on impact was too bright to look at. Even Fuse turned her head away. When the brilliance faded, Randy was wearing a green jersey with the number ten on it, a silver cape, black pants, and tall metal cyborg boots. He was not so stunned by his transformation as Ru was. "I mean, a jersey wasn't what I was expecting for a superhero, but whatever." A devious grin spread across his face. "What's my power?"

"You are the Skaeya of Light."

Randy's enthusiasm left in a hurry. "Light?" he scoffed. "Ru gets like lightning and tornadoes and stuff, and I get *light?*"

Ru hadn't given much thought to her elemental potential. She imagined summoning a big storm, and picked up the grin Randy had dropped.

"Randy, is it?" Fuse asked. To her credit, she didn't seem annoyed at all like most people did when Randy threw a tantrum.

Randy crossed his arms and gave Fuse his toughest look. "Yeah."

"Your clothes right now are similar to what you normally wear, based on what you think you should look like. When you are a full Skaeya, it will change. As for the power of light, it is wise not to underestimate *any* element."

Randy grumbled, but had no arguments. Fuse approached Colleen. "Would you like to try next?"

Colleen jumped. There was a panic in her eyes that Ru didn't understand. Colleen was normally nervous around strangers, but this was something beyond even what an alien should have inspired.

"What's your name?"

Colleen's mouth worked.

"Sorry? I didn't hear you." Fuse inched closer.

Colleen trembled and gripped her pendant with both hands. "I-I can't be a guardian."

Fuse looked concerned but unbelieving. "Why not?"

"I mean, she is kind of a coward," Randy cut in.

"She probably has a more useful power than yours," Ru snapped.

Colleen swallowed. Her voice was barely above a whisper. "This necklace can't be what you think it is. My mother left it to me. I've had it since I was a baby."

Fuse's eyes widened. "May I see it?"

Colleen handed over the pendant and backed away. Fuse's prismatic eyes hardened as she sunk into deep thought. Her gray lips pressed together. "Strange," she said at last. "I have no doubts this *is* a Skaeya pendant. But you should have obtained it recently."

Ru gasped, then burst out, "Was her mother a guardian too?"

Fuse shook her head. "It wouldn't matter if she was or not, each pendant is supposed to be unique to the guardian."

"Oh." Ru deflated a bit, but her mind was already running away with other possibilities. "Maybe the same person who gave us our pendants switched Colleen's mom's pendant out sometime. I don't know how because you wear it all the time," she said to Colleen, "But I don't know how I lived through getting hit by a meteor, either."

Fuse handed the pendant back with a smile. "Just try switching. It won't hurt you."

Colleen's mouth formed the words, but Ru couldn't even hear a whisper. "You're too quiet," Fuse said. "The meteor isn't receiving your command. Try again."

Ru suspected Colleen was distracted by something, but couldn't imagine what. "It's pretty cool. C'mon, let's see what your power is!"

"Yeah!" Randy gave her a thumbs up.

Colleen huffed, breathed deeply, and screamed louder than Ru had ever heard her scream before. "SWITCH METEOR!"

The air grew cold. Snowflakes filled the air, glistening in the pink light from the approaching meteor. It seemed to hit in slow motion. Ru felt frozen in place. She caught a glimpse of Colleen's strangely empty eyes just before impact.

When the snow blew away, Colleen appeared hunched over. Her dewy eyes darted all around. Her uniform had become a sparkling pink dress with a short, flared skirt. She wore white gloves with lacy gauntlets and a belt with a big fluffy bow on the back, tied with a huge white gemstone. Her headband now had a white wing and crystal snowflake pinned above each ear. "Wow," Ru breathed. "Yours is pretty!"

"What is this?" Colleen whimpered. "Why does everything feel so strange?"

"You're awakening to the system," Fuse said.

Randy was yelling, somewhere more distant than he had been. Apparently he'd already lost interest in whatever Colleen would be. "Light power! Shine!"

"That won't work yet," Fuse called to him, amused. "We'll start practicing that when you're all armed."

The group looked at Jayson. He was leaning against a tree, arms tightly crossed, hat pulled down over his eyes. "That's my brother, Jayson," Ru said. "He thinks he's dreaming."

"How am I not?" Jayson said. "This is impossible."

"He's a chicken," Randy sneered.

"That doesn't work on me," Jayson replied coldly.

Ru walked closer. "C'mon, you're next."

All coolness evaporated. "Um, *no*, I don't have to do this. You guys, don't you see it? Something isn't right here!"

"If you think you're dreaming --" Fuse started.

"SWITCH METEOR!"

Fuse jumped.

"There, you happy?" Jayson glared at the sky. "I don't *have* to do this. I didn't say I won't."

Ru grunted in annoyance, but had no time to speak. Hot winds poured in from the sky. Flames burst from the ground as the meteor struck. She was surprised none of the trees ignited.

Jayson stepped out of the fire. He had kept his hat, but the Sox logo had vanished and was no longer dusty and frayed. He wore a black jacket with a four-point star in red on the left side, black pants and shoes. But Ru couldn't see the rest --

"Dude, your shirt's on fire!" Randy yelled.

Jayson looked down, yelped, and batted frantically at the yellow flames that had engulfed his entire shirt.

"Stop drop and roll!" Ru shrieked.

Colleen pulled at Fuse's shirt. "How do I use ice? Quick!"

It was then that Ru noticed Fuse didn't seem worried at all, and Jayson stopped rolling in the sand a minute later. The fire apparently wasn't hurting him, it seemed to be a part of his new shirt. The flames faded significantly as Jayson rose to his feet and dusted himself off.

"It's clear what your power is, correct?" Fuse said with a smirk.

"I hate you," Jayson replied in a level voice.

Fuse grinned, gave them all an approving glance, then closed her eyes. An undercurrent of energy radiated from her feet, into the ground, spreading and circling the entire planet beneath them. "The Lraenu do not realize we are here. I have time to grant you another ability."

"I get to learn how to shoot lasers now?" Randy made a finger gun.

"Flight," Fuse said.

Ru didn't think Randy's face could light up any more, but it did. She felt a flutter of excitement herself. "We can *fly?*"

"Skaeya-cyu means 'flying fighter' -- it's not just a name. I hear Skaeyan humans often dream they can fly. It's because they *know* they can. They were made to forget."

"By who?" Jayson demanded.

Fuse eyed the stars. "I -- don't actually know," she admitted. "It happened long before my time. Perhaps long before the System's time."

Jayson was not about to let it go so easily. "And what exactly do you mean by the System? You say it differently than -- I mean -- well, we can't be outside the system like you said, because Earth is in a galaxy, right? On the edge of one, anyway."

"The System is more than the physical location of the stars," Fuse started.

Randy waved a hand between the two of them "Um, excuse me? We were about to learn how to fly, and you want to sit here and talk?"

Fuse laughed and looked to her left. There was suddenly something there. An enormous, shadowy, but familiar presence overwhelmed Ru's mind. She knew who it was before they stepped out of the trees. The red of their cloak was fiery in the meagre starlight.

"You!" Randy exclaimed.

"This is Ember," Fuse said. "They are the Council's guardian. They can help you remember."

Ember moved no closer, but Ru felt her eyes being drawn to that void where their face should have been. Her eyes and mind focused in an uncomfortable way. Then, a click. A door opened. That weightless feeling came flooding back, that rush of previously unfathomable freedom. She bolted forward and leapt into the air.

Her feet never touched the ground.

"It worked!" Randy yelled.

She heard him grunt and a heavy thud as he landed face-first in the sand. "Ember has to teach you first. You'll know when you've remembered." Fuse smiled up at Ru. "I knew you would learn quickly."

Ru kicked at the air and tried to draw herself forward with her hands, but she only made herself rotate in place. "It isn't like swimming," Fuse said. "The easiest way to start is picturing yourself going where you want to go."

Ru's eyes went straight to the sky. Pink starlight gleamed beyond the silhouettes of palm leaves. Fuse waved a hand at her. "Go on, try it out! Just don't go far, and if you see or feel anything wrong, come back right away."

The air was less dense above canopy. Ru started up slowly, taking in the full breadth of the elegant, sparkling skies. The air swirled lightly around her, tossing her hair but keeping it out of her face. There was no fear as the ground swept away from her. This was where she belonged.

A vast field of alien palms lay beneath her, blue and feathery in the night, littered with tiny, glistening yellow lights. Beyond, there was an ocean, a perfect crystal reflection of the brilliant arc of fuchsia stars near the horizon. The sheer size of the yellow moon nearby left Ru breathless, especially compared to their single, pale-faced moon at home. The more she sighted, the more she could feel. Every single star had its own energy. She felt like she was glowing herself.

"Wow," she heard Colleen sigh.

Ru hadn't realized she'd stopped. The others were drifting her way. She didn't even need to look at them to know, they had a place in her mind too. Jayson flickered, Colleen shimmered, Randy blazed, Fuse beamed. The full sky overwhelmed them all. Ru recalled the sky of her home planet, perfect blue, crystal white, wild, seething gray and black, and knew she would never look at it the same way again.

Fuse's wings hummed loudly as she drew near. "The bulk of your training will take place at the Council's complex," she said, "but the only gatestone from Skae leads here. You will have to come to Iresca before you transfer there."

There was a strange implication in the bird's voice. It was hard to tell what she was looking at. Ru squinted at the shoreline running off to the horizon. At first, she saw nothing but the thorny silhouettes of trees. On a second sweep, something caught her eye. It was very far away, but it was square and unnatural. She thought she could pick out its signal from all the others she was receiving, like a single line of smoke rising into the sky. "What's that?"

Fuse knew exactly what Ru had found. "That is a Lraenu hive. You must keep clear of it until you are well-prepared."

"What? Where is it?" Randy flew higher. "That's the bad guys, right? I'm ready, let's get em!"

"You are not ready," Fuse said gently, "But I am going to send you home now. Especially when your powers are new, you must return to Earth to keep them strong."

"Our powers are like a battery?" Jayson scoffed. "How are we supposed to protect galaxies if we have to stay home all the time?"

"You will see. Return tomorrow night and I will guide you to the Council's complex."

"What if the Lraenu are here waiting for us?" Colleen said fearfully.

"You must be prepared at all times," Fuse warned. "They can travel to Earth. You have a few advantages there -- your power is strengthened and theirs is weakened, and you have allies on your planet watching over you. Eventually, though, you must learn to defend yourselves."

They summoned their meteors again to change back into normal. Fuse lead them to the gatestone with a few words of encouragement, then they were on their way home. Ru's sneakers touched down lightly, as if she was still part of the air, part of the fog that had collected in Tanager Park sometime during the night. The park had been so striking when they'd left the planet, now it was just old. Quarterhill's backyard. The Quarterstone, the gatestone, was no longer illuminated.

"This is *awesome*," Randy exclaimed.

Jayson's eyes were hidden under the brim of his hat, the corners of his mouth turned sharply downward. Colleen clutched at her pendant, which had returned to its original dolphin shape. Ru's head was spinning, but Randy's enthusiasm was contagious. They had powers. They could *fly*. They had just met an *alien*, of all things. Was it real?

Blue light illuminated the hedges. The Blue Star and Ember were near. There were four bracelets in Ember's hands. They swept closer and fastened one around Ru's wrist. Without understanding, she touched it, and gasped as symbols appeared in the air above it. The others gathered around her, even Jayson looked intrigued. "What is this?"

"These are each copies of a book of Accilean legend and prophecy, written before the system came into being," the Star explained. "Learning the Accilean language will help you master your abilities, and we hope, in turn, you may help us better understand its contents."

Ember handed out the other bracelets as Ru poked the symbols. The symbols scrolled sideways with her finger, rows disappearing on the right and more appearing on the left. "I've never seen this language before," she protested. "How will we know where to start?"

"It will come to you." The Star's voice was soothing. "The Accilean language is a little different from any of Earth's. Anyone can understand it when it is spoken, but to read, write, or speak it takes practice."

"Anyone can understand it?" Ru repeated. "How? Like pictures?"

"You never noticed that I am not speaking English?"

All four pairs of eyes snapped to the Star. "Say something again," Randy said slowly.

It was true. The words that whispered from the Star's tranquil flames were unlike anything Ru had heard before, yet the meaning of the words stood out to her instantly. "You understand now. Return home. Come back to the stone at midnight."

The Star winked out. Ember was gone with it.

"Like I need extra homework," Randy said. "At least it'll give us powers. Hey, you don't think these things can *break,* do you? Let's throw it in front of a car and find out."

"This is why they gave you *light* powers. You guys know we gotta keep this a secret, right?" Ru said.

Randy rolled his eyes. "Yes, Mom."

"Dude, we all know you'd be the first one to call down your meteor if you were about to get in another fight with Joe," Jayson said. "Seriously, they said the Lraenu are here, and it's probably better if they don't know who we are."

Colleen's voice quavered. "We don't know what *they* look like."

"Hopefully we don't need to know yet," Ru said. "Fuse said to come back tomorrow night. What time are you guys' parents usually asleep?"

They decided on a time to meet, then rushed home. Ru noticed she wasn't the least bit tired. She and Jayson talked about the bracelet books on the way -- they didn't want their mother to find the books by accident, but she was rarely around to take care of the house anyway, so it wasn't likely she'd stumble across them.

"But I guess aliens would explain all the weird stuff that happens in Quarterhill," Ru whispered.

"Or dreaming," Jayson said flatly. "I'm going to try and sleep."

"How can you? There's no way I can." Ru was about to take her pendant off, hesitated and left it hanging around her neck. "Hey Jayson? Just because you think it's a dream, it doesn't mean you can't play along, right? Why wouldn't you want to be a superhero?"

Jayson paused at the door. "Flying *is* pretty cool. I just don't trust the bird. I think she was hiding something."

"Like what?"

"Who knows? Since we're dreaming, we might never find out. Good night."

Chapter 16 ★ ★ ★ The Hive

An opaline beam of light split the clear Irescan sky. It burned upwards into space and unraveled, vanishing into the starlight. Kestrel's hands tightened into fists. He was almost certain Shryke had let it come to this point on purpose.

There was movement beneath his feet, under the rough stone roof of the base, the "hive" as the Accileans called it. An accurate name, he had to admit. He'd seen beehives on Earth before. He did not know if bees were as mindless as the drones swarming beneath him, but bees were more placid, for certain.

A calling, a warning bell rang in the back of his mind. He stood automatically and jumped from the ledge. He sensed where the drones were all concentrated, reached out, and caught a ledge above a window. Had he truly been human, it would have been a dangerous maneuver, and there was still pain that jolted through his arm when he came to such a sudden stop. But at the moment they all needed to work on having any advantage they could get.

He dropped inside the window and brushed his thin blue hair out of his eyes. The next chamber, a vast, round, high-ceilinged room, only had a door on either side. He could see the drones' eyes flickering, twisted lines of violet and gold and red glowing ominously in the dark. There were hundreds above his head. They would drift like fish, making circles in their murky aquarium, until they were energized. As Kestrel crossed into the room, only visible by the light reflected behind him, the drones stopped cold. He would have admired their discipline if he'd known they had a choice. He was a magnet to their lurid eyes. Only those with more than one tail could concentrate their attention on something else.

The drones flowed around him as he walked to the center of the room. He stared up, reaching out with his mind, hooking into them. He chose ten, nine tailless "stubs" and one a bit more advanced, and moved them close, as easily as moving his own arm. His voice rapped the walls. "A new generation of Skaeya have just opened their eyes. You will guard the gatestone, as close as you can get, lure them far enough away to intercept. They must not be allowed to see the Council." His next order had the more sentient among them exchanging glances. "I want them alive."

The ten left immediately. He released the remaining drones from his command, though they would not stop watching him until he left the room. "Commanders," he barked.

Sylph, her curiosity just barely hidden in the sinister glow of her eyes, swam down to him. Several more followed, tails twining. "Human forms," Kestrel said shortly, then motioned for them to follow to the next room.

Negative light flashed, and the sound of unsteady footsteps filled the air. Kestrel found Shryke in the next room, already in human form, hurriedly stuffing something into his mouth. Kestrel's temper flared, but he kept his voice cold. "The Skaeya are now aware of their true nature and this is how you spend your time?"

"Hey." Shryke waved the scrap of sandwich still left in his hand. "A good burger is never a waste of time. You should try one once."

Lightning flashed. The burger disintegrated into ash. Shryke stared at its remains, then shrugged. "Since I already ate most of that you only owe me two dollars."

Kestrel rarely asked drones to assume human form as it disoriented them, but the commanders valued a free mind and were often more useful that way. They were dressed in Skaeyan clothing that suited their primary tasks. Merlyn the weaponsmith and Kyte the controller wore military camouflage. Karacara the recruiter had a sharp suit and skirt, and Sylph had her usual tight black catsuit for sneaking around. "Where is Pi?" Kestrel question.

Merlyn crossed his heavy arms and snorted. "Who cares?"

"K, you ask every time, and he's never here," Shryke said. "And I don't think any of us actually *want* him here."

The others nodded, and Kestrel had to admit he was not all that displeased himself. "As it is. From this moment forward, we are only to make appearances on Skae in public view. The Caere has been attacking unprovoked."

The commanders' responses ranged from mild shock to annoyance. "Why is it attacking now?" Kyte asked.

"That is precisely the question I intend to answer, which is why I am not restricting you from the planet entirely. It is useless for us to hide from the Accileans, including the Caere, because they can sense who we are even in human form. We appear as a distinct aural void to them, according to Shryke's source." Kestrel eyed Shryke, who nodded to confirm. "However, because Skae is dormant, they do not wish to be known to the general populace and will not attack in the presence of bystanders. By conducting our investigations in close proximity to dormant people, we may limit the Accileans' interference."

He touched the bandaged hilt of one of his swords. "Unfortunately, this will not rule out all confrontation. You risk deconstruction at the hand of the Caere in your true form, and severe injury as a human. In preparation for this, I am to train you to use your abilities in human form. Your extraphysical abilities will be difficult to learn this way, but this knowledge may save your life. It is important to remember that when we are human, we have their weaknesses."

The commanders looked skeptical. Shryke was starting at a small piece of paper in his hand. Only Sylph seemed truly concerned. Kestrel continued. "Their bodies and souls are damaged merely by our language. You are somewhat protected from your own speech, but --"

He inverted his speech. It was difficult to speak properly, his Accilean body rejected the horrific sounds before he could shape them, and the taste they left in his mouth nauseated him. But the effect was exactly what he had intended. Sylph went rigid, screaming in pain. Shryke swore and clawed at his ears. Even the giant Merlyn was doubled over.

"My apologies," Kestrel said gravely, looking specifically at Sylph. "I advise against speaking that way at all on Skae -- its effects are useless on Skaeya as their Axles protect them from its effects. But if you do, make sure you have no Accilean-form allies nearby."

He waited for the commanders to regain their composure. Shryke's eyes were especially venomous, but Kestrel knew he wouldn't be so foolish to counterattack.

"Can we fly on Skae?" Karacara asked.

"Not in human form," Shryke answered before Kestrel could. "There's a seal there that affects us. Thought I'd tell you before K threw you off a building to show you."

Kestrel suppressed his laughter, though a grin escaped. "Even I don't know how to break that," he admitted. "Our elemental control is limited as well, and like our language, it can damage your human form. A Skaeya's element does not touch them because they can give it very specific instruction through the Accilean language. The Accilean elements resist us, therefore we must assert strict control over them. Until you have mastered that, it is best to choose a point of manifestation that is not touching your body, like a weapon."

Shryke shrugged. "I dunno, dude. I don't think most of us have elements that are that useful, at least against the Caere. I mean, what *is* that thing, anyway? They call it the Blue Star on Earth, but obviously it's not actually a star or else the forests it lives it would be starting on fire way more often. My shadows can't do anything against something that's made of light. Sylph already proved her poison doesn't work on it."

"I suspect what is happening on Skae concerns more than the Skaeya and Caere. At the same time, something is different about these particular Skaeya."

"You mean besides that they're little kids? They probably don't know any more than we do."

Kestrel frowned. "No, they would not. That is not the Accileans' way. They are very young, though, and they may be influenced towards our cause, which as primarily why I want them captured rather than killed."

"And who's going to babysit them? Not me."

Lightning sparked at Shryke's feet. He jumped, then hurried away.

Chapter 17 ★ ★ ★ Trouble in Iresca

Ultimately Ru decided against bringing the wristbook to school. It could be stolen, she couldn't actually read it in class, and as much as she hated to admit it, Randy did have a point when he said they didn't know how fragile it was or if there were more of them. She made it a point to ask that night.

School was both easy and difficult. Somehow, she easily finished her homework in study hall, which was rare, and especially surprising when all she could think about was Iresca and her new powers. What would they learn that night? Who was on the Council, and what was their complex like? Was it in another galaxy altogether? What sort of aliens would they meet?

Colleen was less enthused. Ru convinced her to walk home so they could talk a bit more. Colleen was supposed to go straight to Breckenridge on the bus, but she had bigger things to worry about. "Did you find anything in that book?" Colleen asked.

Ru watched leaves tumble across the road. "Nothing," she said at last. "I don't even know where to start. I don't know any of the letters in there. I was going to ask Fuse for help."

"What are these 'Lraenu' he said we're supposed to fight?" Colleen's trembling voice stumbled heavily on the Accilean word. "I think your brother's right to be suspicious. Why us?"

"Why not us? There's a lot of super heroes our age on TV. I can see why they'd pick Randy for sure." Ru rolled her eyes. "Did you see him at recess?"

Some of Colleen's anxiety dissolved in a giggle. "He was running around pretending to fly."

"Jayson had to remind Randy that superheroes have secret identities. But we don't wear masks or anything like that."

"Would anyone believe Randy if he said he was a real superhero?"

Ru shook her head. "If we heard about a meteor hitting school, though, we'll know what's going on."

They passed the east entrance of the park. The big crowds were finally here. Black and orange banners announced the Tanager Park Halloween Festival in letters that looked like dripping ink. The festival was officially the last ten days of October, but with all the people in the park it looked like the party was already underway. The music lineup posted was mostly local artists, but Ru was excited to see that the Shaddow Puppets was the headliner. They really were getting to be a big name.

Ms. Hadley never went to the festival, but she always let Ru and Jayson go and gave them a little money to spend. They usually went with the Fresnel family, which was not a tradition Ru intended to continue when she was old enough, but at least Randy's parents were far less annoying than Randy himself. Gary Fresnel was a junk food fanatic and always looked for the strangest and most outrageous concoctions to be found at festivals. Rachel Fresnel, a bulky, muscular woman just barely taller than her son, was always up for games and any physical contests she could get into. Both had perpetual smiles, even when they were angry -- and Ru had seen them angry with Randy a lot. The family had moved to Quarterhill when Randy was a baby, drawn by the legends that made the town infamous.

"You never know what people will believe here, though," Ru added as an afterthought. "We don't know who we can trust except Fuse and the Blue Star."

"Can we really trust them? We don't even know them."

"Fuse wasn't lying about the power she gave us."

"Did you feel different after you transformed? When I was a Skaeya I was noticing all these things I never did before. It's not the same on Earth."

Ru remembered it well, especially when she thought of the Irescan starscape and the cold spike of the Lraenu hive. "It must be what Fuse meant when she said our planet isn't in the Accilean System. Either that or it's only a power we get when we're transformed."

"I wonder --" A diesel engine rumbled behind them, and Colleen's head jerked up. No bus, only an old truck. "I wonder if we had this power all along, actually. You being able to predict the weather, and my dreams. I -- um -- you remember that dream I had the other week, with the aliens? The one who was killed was Fuse."

"No way!" Ru exclaimed. "Are you sure? Why didn't you say anything before?"

"I wasn't sure at first." Colleen pulled a folded piece of sketchbook paper out of her case. "I drew her after the dream though."

It was out of proportion and sketchy, but Ru could see the resemblance. The way Colleen captured the terror on her face made Ru's stomach roil. "What about the guy who killed her? Did you draw him?"

"Misty has it."

"Can you get it back?"

"I can draw another one." Colleen shuddered. "I'll never forget what *he* looked like. I bet he was a Lraenu. He was definitely some kind of monster. He looked human, but he was a monster."

"We should definitely tell Fuse, then."

"I don't know if it'll do any good. I haven't been able to change my dreams before."

The voice was barely loud enough to reach Ru's ears, but what was said was enough to silence her argument and bring her to a halt. "Skaeya."

It was the anti-tourism guy, the one Ru's mother had said was a war veteran. Ru could easily believe he'd been a drill sergeant, with the way his voice normally carried. Ru could feel the man's eyes boring into her. "Did he just say Skaeya?" Colleen whispered.

"I told you to bury it," the man said in a voice as hard as his expression. "It's not too late."

Ru's curiosity had well overcome any intimidation she felt. "What do you know about it?"

Another diesel engine rumbled. Colleen yelped as the school bus flew past and dashed away. "Hey, wait!" Ru called after her.

"I have to get to the house before they do!"

Ru glanced back at the man's house just in time to see the front door shut. She would never be able to close the gap between herself and her friend -- Colleen had a very long stride -- but she wasn't about to confront the man alone. She took off after the bus.

"How'd you guys get out of your house without anyone seeing?" Randy's voice was small in the murky air, but cheerful.

Jayson scoffed. "Mom is never around. It'd take her a month to notice if we never came home."

Ru knew very well that their mother looked in on them first thing when she came home late from work. It occurred to her, though, that there was no look-in the night before. If Ms. Hadley had come home before they did, she'd have noticed they were missing.

There was a chill in the air, and though Ru knew it wasn't that cold, she felt as if the grass should be covered in frost. The southern sky was pure darkness. Normally, light pollution annoyed her with the way it blocked the stars and spoiled the creepy atmosphere of Tanager Park, but this sky-wide void at the edge of her vision was a little *too* creepy for her. She felt a little more secure when they were covered by the hedge tunnel to the Quarterstone.

"What about you?" Randy poked Colleen, who jumped and squealed.

"I saw them lock the front gate. I *saw* them. But it was open when I touched it. No one asked where I was last night, no one saw me leave. Ru, no one even noticed I wasn't on the bus. If one of the others knew I walked home, they would have told the house mothers for sure."

A flicker, off to the southwest. Ru's eyes darted that way but took in nothing but dark fog. Her heart jumped to life. Someone with a flashlight, she assured herself, but a thought lodged firmly in the back of her head. It was possible that not all the legends were explained by the fact that there was a gateway to an alien world in the park. She shivered and buried her nose in the collar of her jacket.

"I tripped on my way out," Randy said.

"Sounds like you."

"Shut up. It was really loud. I knocked over a lamp! The weird thing is, Mom and Dad were in the other room and didn't even look. I thought for sure Dad would be going for the gun."

"Dude, ask your dad if we can borrow it," Jayson said. "Maybe it can help us against whatever we're fighting."

"For real? C'mon, we have powers!" Randy grinned. "I could have *laser guns* in my fingers, and you could have a flamethrower. That's way better than some weak shotgun."

"Yeah, but we haven't learned to use our powers yet."

Ru expected him to add something about how they were all dreaming, but he never did. Maybe he'd taken her words to heart.

The stone was quiet and dark when they approached this time. There was some debate as to whether it would work. As soon as Randy finally goaded Colleen into stepping up onto the stone with the rest of them, white light winked on, then prismatic fire flared up around them. Ru paid special attention to it now that she knew what was happening, but aside from the light there wasn't much to pay attention to. One second they were in the park, the next they were stumbling off the edges of the stone in the Irescan forest.

Before her eyes could adjust, light flashed through the trees, a stream of thin, shimmering rainbow light. As Fuse passed, she yelled, "Skaeya, switch meteor! NOW!"

Something lunged out of the bushes and slammed right into Fuse. She hurtled off-course and straight into a tree trunk with a sickening *THWACK*. Her light dimmed sharply as she slid to the ground and settled into a limp pile of feathers.

There was sharp cold, the same empty feeling Ru had when she looked at the southern sky moments ago, only amplified. The coldest winter she'd been through couldn't compare to it. But it wasn't just the aura that froze her to the bone. She could see the creature now. Its glowing violet cat eyes illuminated its can-shaped body clearly.

Chapter 18 ★★★ Crash

"What is that?" Randy's eyes were wider than Jayson had ever seen, and he was actually backing away. Randy never backed down.

Jayson was the first to come to his senses. "Switch meteor!"

The others echoed him. Light fell from the sky in a flurry, fire, wind, and snow stunning the monster that had attacked Fuse. A moment later, the Skaeya stood ready to face it.

Only now there were ten.

"It's like all the marshmallows I've ever eaten have come back to haunt me," Randy squeaked.

The red one in the middle had a long pair of tails that twitched eagerly, a snake coiled to spring. "Skaeya," it rasped.

Jayson cringed, but the voice didn't shred his ears this time. His pendant thrummed and that was all. Now that he was transformed, these things seemed to radiate a sharp, very distinct, cold emptiness. It was overwhelming, repulsive, and strangely motivating. Vividly, he remembered the first time he'd seen creatures like this, hovering in his own kitchen, but somehow, they were clearer and easier to see here. He glanced over at Ru and found her eyeing him meaningfully.

An aura flared up around the creatures, a bonfire of negative energy. Pressure built in the air. Ru shot up into the sky, and the others scrambled into the air after her. Jayson just barely managed to hang onto serenity by picturing himself safe and asleep in his room.

Colleen screamed, some twenty feet below the rest of them. "Whoa!" Randy shouted.

A soundless explosion fanned out beneath them, bending the trees down. The icy wind from the shockwave made Jayson want to curl into a ball, but he couldn't take his eyes away. The creatures were riding their own energy, winding their way up into the sky faster than Jayson ever wanted to believe such bulky things could move.

"Yeah, c'mere!" Randy hollered. "I burn a hundred of your little brothers in campfires every year, what are you gonna do about it?"

He dived right at them. Jayson's first reflex was to yell at him to stop, but he was glad someone was doing *something*. Colleen was still flying upwards, and Ru was as frozen as he was, her vivid blue eyes darting all around.

Randy delivered a kick to one of the creatures that sent it spiraling back towards the ground. The other creatures immediately surrounded him, and both Ru and Jayson flew towards them. The creatures scattered. In most dreams, Jayson had to struggle to stay in the air, and he was grateful that flying came easier here.

A green marshmallow sprung right up in his face. He didn't even have time to stop. Negative light engulfed his vision. He was overwhelmed by cold, boneless and void on the inside. His mind reeled, his eyes would not clear no matter how he blinked. The wind cut past him and he realized he was falling. At least this dream was over. Any moment now, he'd be sitting up in bed laughing about this whole ridiculous long nightmare. The palm leaves slapped at him as he plummeted past.

But there was no impact. The next thing he was aware of was his head resting on the sandy ground, two marshmallows hovering over him. Their feline eyes examined him carefully, and though he wanted anything to get away, the cold anchored all parts of him. He was barely aware of his body, he only knew it was there because his hair and hat brim were still in sight. He was so thoroughly frozen he wasn't sure if he was breathing.

Thick thoughts floated through his mind. Dream. They couldn't hurt me if they wanted to.

To his surprise, one of the creatures barked something, and both flew away, leaving him in the sand. He was relieved until he saw them split off and add to the numbers chasing his friends. He could barely see through the broad palm leaves, but even without using his eyes, he somehow knew what was happening, where everyone was. In his mind there were pinpricks of cold energy circulating with clear colorful starlight, his friends. Randy was nearby, wrestling fiercely with one and lashing out at all the others when he had a free limb. Ru twisted and swooped through the sky, graceful and elusive as a swallow, but there were too many close calls with four of them now after her, all firing that freezing energy. Colleen kept going further and further away. Jayson wanted to call to them for help, but even if he was capable, he knew it would be a bad idea with all of his friends being chased. None of them would know how to unfreeze him anyway.

A light flared and blinded him. Rainbow light. His brain tried to say Fuse's name, but his mouth did not obey. The little bird perched on his chest, her natural light dimming enough for Jayson to see her tiny, glittering feathers bristle. She lay flat and looked him in the eye, and her light flashed again. The cold vanished. Jayson bolted upright, knocking Fuse into the air. "What happened? What's going on?"

Randy crashed down beside them, a strangely empty look in his eyes. Fuse darted over to him. Sparkling white light engulfed Randy's whole body. He sat up and shook his shaggy head. "Hey!" he shouted, startling Fuse away. "That was the one I took a bite out of! It's whole again!"

Jayson blinked. "The one you *what?*"

"Well punching 'em wasn't working!"

"They are Lraenu!" Fuse's colorful light churned furiously. "You are lucky they merely immobilized you. They cannot be destroyed by physical attacks. They will regenerate."

"Then how do we win?" Randy demanded.

The bulk of the Lraenu were focusing their efforts on Ru. Colleen had stopped more than a mile away, the Lraenu no longer in pursuit. Jayson could not tell if she was frozen. Ru was fighting instead of just dodging now, but even though he saw no fear, Jayson was sure she'd never thrown a serious punch in her life. Her left arm dangled in an odd way. Randy bristled at the sight of the Lraenu and shot back into the sky. "Wait!" Jayson shouted.

"Listen," Fuse said. "You cannot destroy them when they are in this form. To defeat them, you must change their form. Lraenu are made by corrupting the matter and energy of this universe, whether it be pure energy or actual living things, and many of the living have been changed into Lraenu against their will. You have the power to reverse that corruption. You feel a surge of energy when you transform, yes?"

Jayson nodded.

"Imagine that same energy flowing through you again. Will it back. Concentrate. It is more difficult than flight, but it is the most essential power you have. It is also easier when the Lraenu are close. When you have focused enough that you can see the energy, call out 'crash' and touch the Lraenu. It will revert them."

A body crashed through the palms. Ru hit the ground, the same glazed look in her eyes Randy had when he was frozen. "Lead the Lraenu away," Fuse ordered. "I will teach the others."

Jayson flew up past the Lraenu. As he hoped, they gave a start and swarmed after him. His mind scrabbled for Fuse's instructions. The transformation energy. What had it been like? Fittingly, like a fire, a huge fire. More than a wildfire, more than the fury of all the volcanoes on Earth, a blaze hot enough to match the core of a star. A flame ignited in the back of his mind, then every inch of his skin prickled. The frigid Lraenu aura closing in behind him fed the flame just as Fuse said. At first, he thought the red light around his hand was his imagination, but as the flame grew stronger, he could see it reflecting off the underside of his hat brim, a clear sign that it was not even an afterimage.

He rushed to meet the Lraenu. It wasn't until after he shouted, he realized the word that had come out of his mouth wasn't "crash," but it was the right one. The energy that had been building inside obscured his fist in flames.

It was like punching something that had already been burned. The Lraenu howled and burst into ash and embers. Its howl thinned to a shriek, a panicked squawking, and beyond the plume of ash Jayson saw a feathery, fluttering shape retreat to the trees. *It's just like what happened with the Star and Crowe*, he remembered, *back in the kitchen.*

His skin bristled as cold washed over him. He'd forgotten about the other Lraenu! But before he could react, blue light streaked past him and the creatures evaporated in mid-attack. One became a screeching, spiral-feathered bird, the other merely sparks. Ru circled above, grinning. Randy, a green light trailing behind him like a ribbon, laughed maniacally as he hunted down another Lraenu. In the distance, Colleen flew alongside Fuse. Pink fractals sputtered around her hand, then grew into a steady light. She never had the chance to test her power, though. The Lraenu were gone by the time she returned.

Randy shrugged. "Well, that was easy."

"You did very well," Fuse said, with as much of a smile as a bird could manage.

"It was too easy," Jayson said.

"Ten should be," Fuse replied. "You are the only ones in the galaxies capable of reversing their corruption. There are many, many more Lraenu, scattered throughout the stars. There could just as be thousands the next time you face them."

An uncomfortable silence filled the tropical air. Fuse's bird smile did not dim. "Fear not. You are learning more quickly than I expected. If your Axles awaken soon --"

"Axles?" Ru questioned.

"The meteor that comes to you when you transform is called an Axle. The pendants you wear are small pieces of that Axle. That is how the meteor finds you. It is how you connect to the System, and the source of your power. Once you are fully synchronized with the System, your Axle will awaken, and you will have access to your full power."

"How do we do that, then?" Randy asked eagerly.

"Primarily, you must learn to speak Accilean. Anything can understand it, but learning to speak it is more difficult. It requires an open acceptance of the System. I must admit, I'm surprised Jayson learned it at all, as he thought he was dreaming. Unless I am mistaken and you changed your mind?"

Jayson felt a little hostile for being singled out. "Who says I still don't think I'm dreaming? For all I know, I could be in a coma and can't wake up until we beat the Lraenu."

Fuse shook her head, clearly amused. "Our previous Skaeya were adults, like Jayson suggested. They were too set in their ways to open their minds. They could not learn. They had too many doubts. Your quick learning means you believe in me as much as I believe in you. I am grateful for that."

Ru's smile widened. Jayson was about to make a quip, but suddenly his senses were overwhelmed. All five turned at once towards the Lraenu hive. Nothing looked different. The palm forest swayed placidly, the ocean glittered under intense starlight, but Jayson felt like he was watching a volcano erupt. "What is that?" Colleen whimpered.

Fuse narrowed her eyes. "Go home. More are coming."

Randy smacked a fist into his palm. "We can take 'em."

"No. There is a Commander with them." Fuse's voice was calm, but there was an ominous, agitated buzz in her wings. "You are not ready for him."

The four hurried back to the ground. "Why can't we go the Council's complex? I thought that's where we were going anyway."

"The gatestones have a repulsion field against the Lraenu. Had the four of you remained near the stone, they wouldn't have been able to touch you."

"That would have been helpful to know," Jayson snapped.

"You are here to fight, not hide. But besides the field, Lraenu cannot enter the complex unless we open the gate for them, and this particular Commander is especially dangerous to the Council as well as immune to the field's repulsion effects." Fuse lingered behind, one eye always on the distant hive. "Caere and Ember can protect you on Earth. I will wait until the danger has passed and tell the Council what has happened here. Hurry. They are close."

Jayson didn't want to look back. He didn't have to. He could feel the torrent of icy annihilation headed straight for them. The tension was unbearable, even if it was just a dream. "So Randy," he called, "What do Lraenu taste like?"

"Kind of like dusty styrofoam."

"How do you know what styrofoam tastes like?"

Chapter 19 ★★★ Stakes

The Lraenu drones receded, falling silently and sleekly away, a wave dissolving before it broke. Kestrel scowled as he watched the last of them scatter back into the base below his feet. A few flew off to retrieve what was left of the fallen. Some were gone for good.

Kyte, the drone controller, stood near the edge of the roof. Her fists were at her sides and shoulders stiff, but it was her mind that was working the hardest. The braided tentacles on her head spiked in their ponytail, the tropical wind seemed to surround her, her skin seemed luminous under the vivid pink of the Irescan suns. As the last drone disappeared, the heavy muscles in her arms relaxed. Rough Lraenian curses filled the air.

"I said *follow them*," the man beside her barked in a metal-tinged voice.

"No," Kestrel said sharply.

Pi turned, calm, as if he'd known Kestrel was there all along. Virulent purple eyes stared from deep within the steel plates that slashed his face. As usual, he wore a jacket with the left sleeve torn away, exposing his glassy mechanical arm. It could have been crafted to look organic, but for some reason Pi liked to show off that his human body was falling apart.

"The Skaeya are Sylph and Shryke's domain." Kestrel rested a hand on one of his sword handles. "They do not require your assistance."

The violet metal dominating Pi's face did not shift, but the remaining flesh shaped into a sneer. "Why are the Skaeya still alive, then? You've handled this so ineptly that even though you've known who they are for weeks, you let them gain power. Of course, I shouldn't be surprised that you've let mere children get the better of you."

Kyte cut in. "He doesn't have to explain anything to you."

"He will to Harrier." Pi smirked.

"I am touched by your concern for my well-being," Kestrel said dryly, "but you are not his messenger nor his voice. I wish to speak to Kyte alone."

There was a strange flicker around Pi's fingers, a twist in the air, a tearing. Kestrel did not move, but never looked away from the eye-wrenching energy. Then Pi closed his fist and it vanished. "She could not possibly have anything useful to say. She doesn't have the capacity. But, if you insist."

Pi flashed into his Lraenu form, a tattered, red-eyed wisp, and flew off. Dismissing him from thought, Kestrel approached Kyte. She pulled up one of her tentacles in response to his unspoken question. The end was cut off and dripping pale blue blood. As painful as it must have been, her voice betrayed nothing. "You know I'm not powerful enough to fight him."

"Is that why you failed to capture the Skaeya?"

"No, Commander. I underestimated them. Pi had me send one of the drones after Fuse, but that shouldn't have made a difference."

"Pi could have gotten both of you killed, attacking a Council member," Kestrel said angrily.

"He was probably trying to lure Ember. You know how he is." Kyte quickly transformed into a Lraenu and back again. She was entirely healed. "It's exactly what we thought with the Skaeya, though. They're easier to teach because of their age. We need to act immediately. We should strike at them on Earth, all four of them at once. Caere can't be everywhere."

"I want them *alive*," Kestrel said. "It shouldn't be difficult."

Kyte stared. "Forgive me for questioning your orders -- but why? I mean, not to agree with Pi," her voice reflected her distaste, "but my assessment is that they could become very dangerous, very quickly."

Kestrel gazed at the ocean, silent for a moment. "They have never been this young before."

"That bothers you?"

"We cannot afford to show weakness, the Council will take advantage of it. I agree, these children can be as much of a threat as any Skaeya before them, even more so." Kestrel saw more drones return, empty-handed. "But the malleability of their minds can work in more than one way. If we truly believe in our cause, should we not try to convince others rather than force our way? Especially with the Skaeyans? As of yet they have no stake in the Accilean System, they are not part of it. They are unaware."

Kyte shook her head. "Don't let Pi know you're going soft."

Kestrel glared. Kyte held her hands up, grinning. "Look, personally I think the Skaeyans would never accept us. But if that's how you want to handle them, we'll do it. Except Pi."

"Leave Pi to me."

"I'm just saying, I'm not exaggerating their potential. Sylph says these Skaeya manifested some of their power before they were first armed."

"She mentioned that to me, though she didn't have time to go over specifics."

"She's in Recovery right now, you could just go ask her."

Kestrel looked sharply at Kyte. "She's *here?* What happened to her?"

Kyte looked taken aback by his sudden intensity. "I don't know. No external injuries as far as I could tell."

Without another word, Kestrel headed for the lower levels. The Recovery wing of their base was small and not used often; Lraenu could heal themselves of nearly all injuries, but not everything, and some conditions stopped them from assuming Lraenu form.

The room Sylph had chosen was dimly lit from the narrow window on the west wall. Sylph lay on a padded cot near it, curled as if she were asleep, but she sat up when she heard his footsteps. He noticed a thin chain clutched in her hand.

"Is that one of their talismans?"

Sylph eyed the object in her hand. It was a silver pendant. Her eyes reflected its murky depth as did her voice. "No, mine."

"What happened? You're quite pale. Are you well?"

"No," she said faintly.

She rested her head back on the cot. Kestrel turned to leave. "Has Eurus been in? I will find him."

Sylph's voice caught him before he left. "I'm going back to Skae. What do you want me to do?"

"Nothing," Kestrel said firmly. "Do not return to Skae. You will not be able to access your Lraenu form if you are ill, and Caere might take advantage of that."

"I'm not afraid of her."

Sighing, Kestrel walked over and knelt by the cot. "Your absence will not be noticed at your post, we will make sure of that. Shryke can take over everything else."

Stubborn light appeared in Sylph's eyes. "All Shryke would want to do is waste more time. He'd probably end up being best friends with them and spend the rest of his days at that arcade."

Kestrel grimaced. She was not wrong, exactly. "Sending you vulnerable like this is not worth the risk. I would rather not lose someone who has served with me as long as you have."

She was silent for a long time, and just as Kestrel was about to leave, she spoke up. "It's been a while, hasn't it? We've known each other since before we joined the Lraenu. Do you remember the time before?"

An image flashed to mind. Rain pouring from the sky. Blood and negative light on a dingy street. A man with a demonic smile. A shade of violet deep enough to drown in.

"That time is meaningless now." Kestrel stood. "As far as you and I should be concerned, we have always been Lraenu."

"Commander Kestrel," a soft voice called from the door.

Sylph's eyes went wide, her face grim. Kestrel knew who it was without looking. A man in a sleek, tight black and yellow uniform. His expression was perpetually gentle and innocent, but his presence usually meant something more alarming. "Zephyrus," Kestrel acknowledged.

"Harrier is calling."

Questions were not asked, nor reasons given. Still, Kestrel couldn't help but wonder where Pi had gone.

The hall to the heartroom was long, quiet, and bathed in teal light from the glowing mist that veiled the ceiling. The color was a measure of Accilean Standard time, something Fuse had difficulty keeping track of on a planet without modern technology. She was usually the last to arrive in the Council's complex, often after being reminded by one of her friends. Some people were thrilled about a mere lytra being summoned to represent the entire galaxy, but many had their doubts.

Her footsteps were heavy in the stone-silent hallway, even the swishing fringe of her robe echoed. The first time she'd been down this hall, she'd been awed. She'd never seen any type of artificial construction besides the Lraenu hive, that dull, grey, rough cube that everyone on Iresca knew to keep their distance from, apart from a few of Fuse's more foolhardy friends. The walls and floors of the complex were polished to a mirror shine and lined with swirling, complex patterns that changed with the lighted mist on the ceiling. There were tall doors with ringed seals that tended to open in dramatic bursts of light, and cavernous rooms with windows looking upon colorful nebula clouds and starfields. Usually music could be heard from somewhere in the distance, echoing, never the same kind as most planets had several styles. She had been very young the first time she'd been to the complex, but then again, most of the Council considered her very young now, and given the lifespan of a lytra, probably so for the remainder of her days. She had been called to serve early out of necessity.

Fuse pressed down on the seal to the heartroom door. The seal was half her size and as round as most moons, the symbol a glass rainbow sphere with three rings around it.

The door split open, revealing the heartroom. It had the appearance of a massive platform floating in space, hovering above Galaxy Axest's swirled stars, but Fuse was told there was a barrier of some kind at the edges of the platform. That made more sense to her than a great deal of Accilean technology. Much more sense than the fact that the platform appeared to be lit, but there were no actual lights shining on or from it.

A woman lowered her hood as she approached Fuse. Cutyri's face was lined, though young for her age, framed by long cobalt hair. Her long, tilted eyes were the same vivid blue, and worried, as Fuse would expect today. Two thin black chains dangled from her bangs to her collar, they rang as she moved, with a much more crystalline sound than one would expect from their iron appearance. She moved gracefully, flowing like smoke. "You will be called first," she said.

Fuse stared further down the platform. "I know."

"I have spoken to Odeny, but I'm not certain what actions he will take."

Usually no one knew. it was Odeny's duty as the Council moderator to be as neutral and logical as possible, and even if he couldn't, he was very good at having people come to agreement. It would be the first time Fuse was leading an issue, and with so much at stake he thought it would be better for Cutyri to present their concerns. She had been with the Council since its beginnings. "I don't know if I --"

Cutyri seemed to read Fuse's thoughts. "It must be you. You have the most to lose, and you have the most power to change the outcome." She touched Fuse's shoulder, and even though her touch was as light as a breeze, there was a sudden and thorough warmth that shimmered through Fuse's body. "I would take your place in an instant if that didn't matter."

Fuse smiled weakly. "Thank you."

The door slid open again, a square of teal forming out of the void, and Odeny stepped in. He was a strong but fluid being, humanoid from the waist up, but with an abdomen and legs like a spider. His skin was pale with silver patches, his hair wiry, and his eyes glowed a blank, hot white. With Odeny's arrival, all twenty Council representatives were there, and they formed a circle around the seal in the center of the platform.

Even though Odeny was potentially Fuse's executioner, the sight of him, the way his rich voice wove Accilean words intricately with the light he radiated, emptied Fuse's mind of all nervousness. She had taken an instant liking to him, and it wasn't until years later that she understood why. It had come up in conversation that the amount a light a lytra gave off was a measure of its health. To lytra, light inherently meant good things, energy, happiness, safety, and Odeny was practically made of it. She tried not to let it cloud her focus from then on. It was easier to remember when she found out that some of the Lraenu glowed as well.

"This emergency meeting has been called to discuss future policies in dealing with the Lraenu," Odeny said, after confirming all were present. "Fuse?"

As soon as Fuse set foot on the seal, sparks shot up around her. She gasped as her body was suddenly forced into the form of a tiny bird. Fortunately, she was able to catch the air with her wings, but she wished she hadn't been so absorbed in thought. She lifted herself up so she could be seen by all of her fellow Council members. Given the variety of species here, there were quite a few differences in height, Loch from Galaxy Sylwoth being the largest, and ironically one of the smallest creatures in his galaxy. He was lying on the floor to somewhat even the field. He was fairly placid, but Fuse could not help being intimidated being a fraction of the size of his furry snout.

She was grateful the seal carried her voice so she didn't have to shout. "The Skaeya of this generation are showing tremendous progress. They have already begun to learn Accilean words. They have also encountered drones and defeated them. But we need more time."

A harsh whisper cut Fuse off. "Enough time has passed!"

"Veah," Odeny warned.

Fuse could not see the entity that the voice had come from, at most, Veah's physical form was a vague, glowing mist. Still, he was very good at making himself heard. "The Lraenu have overrun Kelsilde. How long has Ani been missing?"

Fuse put a fierce rein on her temper. Ani was the Council member she'd been chosen to replace.

"Shyra is also severely infected," Veah continued. "Even you, Odeny, have been avoiding entire planets there. Our galaxies are not far behind at this rate."

"It is unwise for any of us to remain near Lraenu when we are not permitted to fight them," Odeny said.

"Then if we really *must* rely on the Skaeya, they should not be chosen from a single planet whose populace is collectively unaware of the System! They cannot be relied on if they can't even comprehend the size of the system we represent."

"Speak to Ember about it, then," Fuse said with an agitated flutter.

"Ember has protected us for centuries," Cutyri pointed out. "Surely we should work with what they give us, or at least consult them? We could have more like the Golden Skaeya at hand, if what Fuse says is true."

The wisp in Veah's voice became more of a hiss. "Ember obviously has the power to defeat the Lraenu, but do they? They are playing games with us. For all we know, they're allied with the Lraenu."

"Do not speak of Ember in such a way," someone else said coldly.

Everyone spoke at once.

"They could destroy us, no matter what side they're on."

"But Veah is right that we must act. The Lraenu have already grown out of our control and we cannot keep pursuing the same course of action."

Odeny had his eyes closed. Likely, he could understand every word spoken at once. Finally, he called for a silence. "You have introduced the Skaeya to the prophecies?" Odeny asked Fuse.

"Ember has."

"We are still waiting for the next sign," he said to the rest of the Council. "The Angel has not yet appeared."

"How long has it been since one of the prophecies has been fulfilled?" Veah's voice was challenging, but it also sounded like an honest question. "The Angel may not even exist."

Cutyri shook her head. "All of them have been true so far."

"This is not a matter to be decided by fear," Odeny stared at Veah, "or promises." He turned his luminous gaze to Fuse. "This is a situation most grave no matter what we decide, and if anything, we should confer with Ember before making a final decision. We should meet these Skaeya as well."

The Council rumbled in agreement. Fuse fluttered over the edge of the seal and out of its range, reviving her human form. Odeny followed. "Bring the Skaeya here as soon as possible. I hope you are not being overly optimistic."

"I mean what I said. But Veah --"

Odeny's people did not smile, but his voice was sympathetic and encouraging. "Do not let him disturb you. He has been with the Council for a long time, but so have many others that agree with you."

Fuse nodded, her smile grim. "As soon as possible," she said.

Chapter 20 ★ ★ ★ On the Way Home

Ru inhaled deeply, her eyes locked on the heavy clouds above. The sharp scent of damp asphalt and freshly fallen leaves was in the air. A drizzle began as she left the school parking lot, a lulling gray mist that put the world around her to sleep. She waved to Colleen as the bus rumbled past. The girls at Breckenridge had noticed none of Colleen's absences, but Colleen didn't want to take too many chances, and decided not to walk with Ru.

Ru's mind had been preoccupied with Iresca all day. She could still feel the rush of soaring through the sky. She could hardly wait to go back. A light breeze kicked up, and she wondered about it. She had always been able to predict the weather. Was it because her element was the sky? Or was she given the sky element because she understood the weather? It was strange to think that she would be able to control something so big. Fighting the Lraenu would sure be easier with the ability to level a tornado at them, though.

The Lraenu looked ridiculous in hindsight, but just the memory of their paralyzing aura sent a shiver through her. When she'd first encountered the ones in her kitchen, she hadn't been awakened and it was terrifying then. As a Skaeya, she could fully sense it and comprehend how powerful they were, but her transformation protected her from being truly affected.

Ru shivered again and pulled at her jacket strings. Away from school, the street was nearly silent. There were no cars, no people out walking their dogs, no other students headed home or to the park. Windows were dark and empty. The rain picked up, glossing the street, rustling the leaves, but the sound did not fill the hollowness around her. It felt wrong. Even with the weather like this, there would still be people headed to the park at this time of year just for the atmosphere.

Suddenly words filled the sour air, vicious words that rattled her entire body without being loud enough to do so. Ru's heartbeat surged as she realized the wrongness had not been her imagination. Hands over her ears, eyes watering, she looked back. A gray Lraenu hovered over the driveway of the next house down. Its burning violet eyes cast a vivid reflection on the rain-slicked street. It sounded almost like it was singing, hypnotic and rhythmic in its own ghastly way. Ru found herself trying to run, but she only strained against solidly immobile feet. Whether it was fear or something the Lraenu was doing, Ru could not tell, but there was only one way out.

"SWITCH METEOR!" she shouted over the noise.

Roaring winds drowned the Lraenu out. It was blown backwards, then silenced as the force of the meteor impact sent it hurtling into a mailbox. Ru dashed out of the swirling residual energy with glowing fists. She swung wildly. Though the Lraenu had tails, each of Ru's strikes missed by inches. The Lraenu spiraled around her, faster than she could turn and just out of arm's reach. Its voice formed recognizable words, still in that horrific parody of sound. "Crashwave has been tried," it mocked.

Ice shot down her spine as one of its tails tapped the back of her head. Her mind went blank and her body went numb. The light faded from her fists as she folded to the ground. The Lraenu scowled down at her.

Angry, frantic thoughts broke through the haze that had settled over her mind. This time Fuse wasn't there to undo the freeze, but there was no way she should have been alone on the street at that moment. *Where are all the people? How did it cut me off from all the people?*

Did the Lraenu kill them?

Would it do that? Of course it would – they were the bad guys, right? Was she too late to protect them? Wasn't that what she was supposed to do?

The urgency that followed that thought cut cleanly through the fog. Her pendant flared with brilliant blue swirls of light. The Lraenu jolted backwards and shielded its eyes with one of its tails. Ru sprang back to her feet, dashed across the nearest lawn, and ducked into a cluster of pine trees. The rain thickened, but strangely, she remained dry. When she looked back towards the street, the Lraenu was gone.

First, she tried to slow the huge, gasping breaths she was taking. The Lraenu could probably hear that, but surely it would have attacked if it knew where she was? She had to find the Lraenu first. As fast as the creature moved, Ru would have to surprise or outwit it if she wanted to catch it with "crashwave," as it had called the attack. Running away was not an option. If it was trying to infect Earth like it had done elsewhere, and she was one of the only people on the planet capable of stopping it, she couldn't let it get away.

It was still on the street, out of visual range, but Ru could pinpoint its aura down to the foot. She tried to remember if Fuse had mentioned how to use her elemental power. *Something called an Axle, right? How do I activate it?* If he'd told her, it was lost in the racing of her mind. But maybe it was already active. She'd just been wondering if she could predict the weather because of some latent power she'd had before transformation. Maybe she could use her power all along and Fuse was unaware. If she could summon lightning, it could set the Lraenu on fire. Fuse said they couldn't be destroyed that way, but setting it on fire might disorient enough to reach it with the crashwave.

She focused on the pouring clouds. She imagined streaks of lightning raining down, the Lraenu sparking and bursting into flames, smoldering in the street. She tried to call back the feeling of weightlessness the came from her transformation. *Wait, no! That's how to summon the crashwave*, she thought in a panic. *The glow will give me away!*

A new plan formed. She couldn't close the distance on foot in time to surprise the Lraenu, but she could fly a lot faster. Could she fly on Earth, though? She stepped into the air, one foot at a time, and remained there. Then, she started to concentrate. If she could bring the crashwave up right before she hit the Lraenu, she might stand a chance.

The world disappeared. Her head snapped around as her feet were yanked out from under her. She sailed high into the air feet first, arms wheeling, and caught one breathless glimpse of the tops of the surrounding houses. Then the void force gripping her ankle slammed her down onto the street.

She tried to scream, but sudden weight on her chest would not allow her to draw breath. Jarring, thorough pain kept her motionless. She felt warmth trickle down her face along with the cold rain. Then, a heavy cord whipped around her neck and wrenched her off the ground. The Lraenu had her coiled in one of its tails. Randy had been wrong, it wasn't like styrofoam at all.

"Don't -" she gasped, just before the tail closed her throat.

She lashed out, scraping the tail with her fingernails. The Lraenu's violet eyes raged in the mist, a steady, malicious stare that darkened her mind even more quickly than the lack of oxygen. Ru's hands fell away, she raised her face to the sky. One last frenzied thought glimmered in her head. The Lraenu was close enough to use crashwave.

The thought bloomed like a firework. Blue light flashed. The tail was gone. Ru dropped to her knees, shaking, choking, her head swimming. Where the Lraenu has been, a black shape stirred on the concrete, much bigger than most birds Ru was familiar with.

The Lraenu shifted, and Ru realized it was a woman. Her silver hair shined intensely under the rain. Her eyes were unfocused. There was a stick at her side with a long blade on the end. "You're -- Sylph," Ru said hoarsely.

The glare Sylph gave curdled Ru's blood. There was a swirl of negative light, and the former Lraenu vanished along with her weapon.

Ru wanted to curl up on the street right where she was. She wasn't sure she could get up, but she had to try. She spared a glance at her body and was relieved there were only a few scrapes that she could see. No obviously broken limbs. Her head was still very fuzzy, though, and her muscles were slow to draw and aching. If the others were under attack at this very moment, she might not be able to help them. But she had to at least warn them. She slowly angled her way to her feet.

There was a small, sharp prickle in her spine, then her back and chest exploded with pain. Never in her life had she felt agony this intense. She tried to scream, and was unable to draw breath. Cold concrete slapped against the side of her face. Sylph appeared out of the corner of her eye, then vanished once again.

The last thing she saw was a small silver figure with wings. It reminded her of an angel figurine her mother kept in the study.

Chapter 21 ★★★ The Solution

Everything was light. No weight, no substance. It was not sleep, not this time. Even she was light. She'd lost her name to it.

When she saw the angel, she had form again, though still no weight. She floated through the air under no volition of her own. The world painted itself out of blinding whiteness, an endless, shimmering sea of stars and iridescent clouds, an ocean, a galaxy, in all the colors she could imagine and even more she could not put a name to. A perfect golden sun was at the center of it all. She felt drawn to it, but the angel's presence kept her where she was.

The angel was no stranger. He had skin and hair as iridescent as the clouds, red and black armor trimmed in gold. Giant, pearly feathered wings curved up over his head. She'd seen him many times before. An old friend. A relief to see after what she'd just been through. What had she been through? She couldn't remember. It didn't matter, it was done.

The angel's startled expression turned to sadness. *No, young one. This is just the beginning.*

The look devastated her. She thought she was crying, but it was hard to tell, being less than air. His shadow crossed her, and he wrapped his arms and wings around her. She could feel the very warmth of the nearby stars with it, all their energy reaching out to her, enveloping her and whispering encouragement in her mind.

Then she was drifting back.

———

Muffled voices created a moody hum in the Council heartroom. An occasional sharp word would rise above, but no severe arguments were sparked. Fuse had a difficult time keeping her own voice down, as it was hard to do with Tourmalyne at times, but she knew she had to be especially careful about what she said at the moment.

Tourmalyne was from Valynahar Graen, the closest represented galaxy to Fuse's own. The Skaeyans Fuse had met called it the Andromeda Galaxy, which had startled her. At the time as she did not know Skaeyans were aware of the existence of galaxies at all, and the methods they had used to discover things beyond what their eyes could see were extremely inventive given their resources. Still, Skae's lack of common Accilean technology was one reason many Accileans looked down on Skaeyans, and even argue that the System's guardians should not come from there -- not like they had a choice in the matter. Ember did what they willed. Tourmalyne was one of the ones who wanted the Skaeya to be chosen from elsewhere.

Tourmalyne was of a planet and species that was very similar to that of Skaeyan humans, but they were generally more elegant, a bit weaker in physical strength, and more of an anti-social nature. Fuse also found that most people she'd met from that planet were strikingly beautiful. Tourmalyne was willowy despite that everything about her seemed to be made of precious stone, from the pure lustrous gold of her hair to the diamond whites of her eyes. The dress she wore, littered with actual gemstones, seemed drab compared to her.

"You picked up right where Ani left off," she said. "Just one more chance. One more. It's good you're carrying out her will, but at some point you will have to make your own decisions."

Fuse frowned. "I did not speak much with Ani. But Skaeyans, I've been around all my life. Might I add, it's easier to detach yourself from the decisions you must make when you're not affected by the results."

There was a spark of anger in Tourmalyne's eyes. "My galaxy is closest to yours. It could very easily affect mine."

"The Skaeya --"

"Forget the Skaeya. You're using a spoon to dig through a mountain."

Fuse suppressed a growl. "And you want to use a mountain to crush a fly."

"The Lraenu are not a mere annoyance." Tourmalyne's fingers tightened on her cup. "If you've had so much experience with them, you should know that."

"I do know that. And I still think the Skaeya --"

The main door slid open. After a short silence, murmurs began anew. Everyone was already here.

Instead of the misty glow of the hall, a sharp white light blared in. All froze, except Odeny, who moved towards the door as if nothing unusual was happening. He let the harsh light meld into his own soft luminescence, reading the intentions of its source. His blank eyes widened. "It's Unity," he announced.

Fuse's stomach plummeted. She couldn't breathe.

The little silver sprite lifted her head at the sound of her name, but looked away just as quickly. A ball of light followed her in, drawing flowing mist after it, following the movement of her hands. She guided it to the center ring, and as it reached the floor, the light wafted away. Ru lay on the seal, pale and motionless. Large, dark patches of blood stained her shirt.

There was absolute silence as the Council surrounded the seal, some staring in horror, some with heads bowed. Fuse shoved her way through, followed closely by Odeny and Cutyri. She reached towards Ru, then yanked her arm back when her hand suddenly sprouted feathers. Cutyri took Fuse's arm and pulled her aside, then stepped into the ring herself.

Veah's voice filled the air with the harshness of a rattlesnake tail. "This is one of the Skaeya?"

"Unity does not bring us civilians." Tourmalyne could barely be heard.

"This is a *child*. Who in their right mind would assign this task to a *child*?"

"Unity was wrong," Cutyri said sharply. "She's alive."

Everyone drew a bit nearer to the seal. Ru stirred, a faint moan humming in her throat.

"Well, don't make Unity right!" Veah ordered. "Switch the girl back!"

"Be careful," Odeny said.

Cutyri reached into the collar of her robe and pulled out a round medallion with the Council's symbol in stained glass. Touching the medallion to Ru's pendant, Cutyri closed her eyes and murmured a few words. No meteors fell; instead, a tiny light shined inside the gem in Ru's pendant, and Ru was instantly in her old street clothes. She lay on her side, still.

The chamber seemed to dim, and startled voices filled the air. Fuse barely noticed. She stood as close to the edge of the ring as possible. Her eyes never left Ru. Finally, she had no patience left. She leapt inside the ring and embraced her bird form, then landed on Ru's upright shoulder. It was then that Fuse noticed something was off. Ru wasn't breathing properly, it was ragged, whistling. Fuse was about to speak up when Tourmalyne cried out, "She's still hurt!"

The pastel blue of Ru's sweatshirt had growing red stains. Odeny skittered to the ring. "That's -- impossible. Reversing her transformation should have healed her."

The Daeneata leader, Tarian, spoke up. She was never difficult to hear, being one of larger members of the council, her deep voice practically shook the non-existent walls of the room. "The ring is known for casting illusions when we need to know something important."

Cutyri touched Ru's shirt. Her fingers came away red and glossy in the dim light.

"I'm curious, Fuse." Veah was somewhere near the back of the crowd, but his wispy voice carried well enough for everyone to hear. "How much protection can a dead Skaeya offer us? Are the other three children as well? Are you willing to let them die just to hold on for a few more days?"

"*Hypocrite*," Fuse snarled, lunging towards Veah. She burst into her human form outside the ring and was stopped by the thick press the others had created. "If we had it *your* way, *all* Skaeyans would die!"

"Fuse?"

The soft whimper came from the ring. Fuse turned back. "Are you talking about me? Please don't let me die. Please?"

Cutyri's expression was grim, but she gently laid a hand on Ru's shoulder and began to summon healing energy. "You'll be all right, young one. Rest."

To Fuse, she turned knowing, cold eyes. "She doesn't know."

Fuse looked like she'd been suddenly caged. "I told them what they needed to know at the time," she said shortly.

"What?" Ru seemed barely awake.

Cutyri's stare was relentless. "You tell her of the Council's plan, or I will."

Fuse bowed her head, then knelt as close to the ring as she could without transforming. "Ru -- I'm sorry, I -- I didn't want to set you back from the start. It's just -- the majority of the Council has no faith in the Skaeya."

"Why not?"

"Almost every Skaeya that has come before you has died at the hands of the Lraenu."

Ru looked like she was quietly processing, but not deterred, and Fuse could barely force out what she had to say next. "The Lraenu are getting far out of control, and their source seems to be Kelsilde. In order to solve the problem -- the Council --" Fuse took a deep breath. "They want to destroy the galaxy."

Ru seemed completely lifeless for the moment, her eyes blank, and it looked like she wasn't breathing. Then she curled into a ball. "Rest," Cutyri repeated in Ru's language, as best she could. "We will help you."

She reached her hand out, but the ring was empty.

Cutyri jumped and blinked her eyes rapidly. A gold feather drifted down in front of her. She reached out to touch it. There were more, spiraling down in a column bordered by the edges of the ring. Motes of light were starting to float up from the floor, fireflies circling up into the sky. Cutyri stood carefully and stepped back. "The ring must be about to show us something about her."

Just as Cutyri came to that conclusion, an enormous pair of wings unfolded out of thin air. Fuse felt a rush of warm raw power burst through the heartroom, which sent exclamations rippling through the Council ranks. The ring showed visions, not sensations.

And then there stood Ru. Only it wasn't Ru -- this person was much older, much bigger, with gigantic gold feathered wings and armor of a deep ocean blue, a long black cape, and radiating more energy than any normal living being should have been. It was more like Ru was only a small part of this person, part of this humanoid star that was slowly turning the light of the heartroom gold.

"The Angel," Odeny said breathlessly.

He knelt on the floor, and the others in the Council immediately followed his lead. Even Fuse, who had only heard of this figure in passing, dropped to one knee and looked on with a mix of awe, fear, and confusion. The ring tended to reveal the true state of who or whatever entered, but she had not sensed a thing like this from Ru before. Was this her true form? Or was something borrowing her?

A voice spoke in clear Accilean, a kind they hadn't heard in a long time, one that pierced through every thought in their minds and drew every ounce of their attention, if it hadn't been focused on the Angel in the first place.

"*We three have been separated by a deep rift in time. We need unity.*"

They waited.

The Angel met Fuse's eyes. A thought crept into the back of Fuse's mind, a truth she had been hoping not to find. Then there was a burst of feathers, and Ru crumbled to the ground. This time, Fuse was the only one who didn't go to help. She flashed into bird form and flew from the room.

Chapter 22 ★★★ Belief

"This is how I know we're dreaming," Jayson said. "Galaxies are thousands of light years across. Do you know how *huge* that is? A light year is how far light travels in a year. Light travels at over a hundred thousand miles per *second*."

"You made that up," Randy snorted.

"I did not, it's in our science book." Jayson pulled the book out of his backpack and flipped to the table of contents. "I'll show you, but think about it. If this Iresca is on the other side of the galaxy, how can we travel all that way in a split second?"

"Magic," Randy said.

Jayson sighed and cradled his head in one hand. "OK. But even if it is. Our galaxy is about a hundred thousand light years across. Multiply that by twenty. Fuse is saying that the four of us are supposed to protect *all of that*. That's impossible."

"Hey, I know light powers aren't the greatest, but you're not giving us enough credit."

"Are you even listening to me?"

Ru wanted to speak up, to tell him that he was right. That Fuse hadn't told them the truth. That it was impossible. But this conversation was in the past, her words would not reach over the distance in time.

She cried out and opened her eyes.

There was an older woman with long blue hair sitting on a cushioned stool near the foot of her bed. No -- this wasn't her bed, or even her room. It was a small chamber with a highly polished floor and walls split by long windows, the glass the only thing between her and an impressive field of stars. The room was filled with some familiar, tall potted plants and flowers, and others not so familiar, but the thick fragrance of them all at once was comforting. The bed looked like a cloud, so full of white fluff she couldn't see the structure underneath, if there was one.

Ru's mind whirled. The last thing she remembered was seeing the Council and intense pain -- she sat up and felt her chest. It was normal.

"Your pendant wasn't damaged, so I was able to use it to restructure your body," the woman said softly. "How do you feel?"

"I -- I don't --" Ru barely had a grasp on words. "I saw you before?"

"My name is Cutyri. I am the representative of Galaxy Kalaedes, and a friend of Fuse." She plucked a bottle from among the plants, and poured a viscous blue liquid into a glass. "Drink this."

Ru hadn't realized until that moment how hollow and hungry she was feeling. She gulped down the drink in seconds, not caring what it was or what it tasted like. Fortunately, it was pleasant, and it brought her mind to life. Cutyru took the glass back, rose from her stool, and took a long staff with what looked like butterfly wings from the corner. She tapped a wing to one of the windows, and something small and bright flitted up to her outside. As Cutyri spoke to it, Ru could feel the unfamiliar Accilean words ripple through the air. After, Ru was somehow able to see the thing at the window, a lightbulb-shaped insect with wings like the ones on Cutyri's staff. Cutyri nodded, and it flew away.

"What is that?"

"A le'at. They are our messengers. Very adaptable creatures, they can withstand the vacuum of space without technological support. We based much of our atmospheric adjustment technology on their biology. I am letting the Council know you will survive, since it seems to be one of the most important factors in a major decision we have to make now." Cutyri moved her seat up to the head of Ru's bed. "Do you remember what Fuse told you?"

A knot tightened sharply in Ru's throat, and tears brimmed in her eyes again. She wanted more than anything for that memory to be a nightmare. "He said you want to destroy the galaxy."

"Not all of us, and not yet. Our situation has become even more complicated." There was a tiny fire in Cutryi's voice that made Ru wonder if she had a plan. "Forgive me for not addressing you in your language. I can understand you, but as you can hear --" she winced as she made an attempt at English. It was recognizable, but she clearly struggled with it. "I om noat os skaeld aen Aenglash aes Fyuss aes."

"I'm supposed to learn Accilean anyway," Ru said. "Though -- I don't see how it matters."

"All hope is not lost. But I will not omit the truth as Fuse did -- your chances of saving your galaxy are slim." Cutyru folded her hands on her lap. "Ember and the prophecies given to you for reference, once told us of an entity called the Angel. This being is embedded somewhere deep in the Accilean System. This Angel was supposed to bring us a message, a clue as to how to save the galaxies should our system be severely threatened. The Angel conveyed this message through you: 'We three have been separated by a deep rift in time. We need unity.' Do you remember that?"

Ru shook her head, and a wave of dizziness made her regret it immediately.

"I believe she was referring to particular artifacts that may have the ability to seal the Lraenu. But no one knows where they are, and the Angel's appearance has thrown the Council into panic. Many say the Angel's appearance is a sign that the galaxies are in extreme danger. The Council as a whole has chosen to give you, the Skaeya, one of your weeks to prove yourself before Kelsilde is destroyed."

"*What?*" Ru's anger fired, dispelling any disorientation left in her head. "The Angel didn't say to *destroy* the galaxy! That doesn't make any sense! Doesn't anyone *living* there get a say in it?"

"Fuse, technically," Cutyri sighed. "Worlds are created and destroyed by no will of our own every day, and the Lraenu are taking that further out of our hands. The Council fears losing what control they have left."

"There's no way you have the power to destroy a whole galaxy," Ru challenged.

"The Accilean System gives us that power."

For once Ru found herself clinging to her doubts, but when she recalled the power that flowed through her during transformation, she could not deny that it could possibly be true.

"The System is supposed to bring us peace and order," Cutyri continued, "to bring us understanding on levels we could never reach on our own. It is our primary duty to maintain the system so the galaxies remain peaceful. But the Lraenu have found a way to corrupt that system along with the galaxies it contains. If they were to completely gain control of the system, it would be even more disastrous than the destruction of a galaxy."

"Then let us fight them!" Ru said. "That's what we're here for!"

Cutyri's eyes were icy. "Why should we believe in you if you don't?"

The words cut deep. Ru couldn't even muster the weakest of denials. Nothing came but tears. "*IT'S NOT FAIR!*" she screamed. "You *can't* do this! You can't kill Mom and Vince and Ms. Graham and even Joe -- tell them to do something else! You're in the Council, they have to listen to you!"

Cutyri was gripping her robes, her expression tinged with pain. "I am trying. I will not give up. But as I said, most of the Council is terrified and desperate. You've felt the Lraenian presence. You feel the void when they are near, the agony they cause when they speak." She gently brushed aside Ru's bangs and pressed a finger to her forehead. "This presence is in the core of your galaxy and has spread mostly throughout."

Ru could feel it. Visually the stars looked the same, a spiral of glitter, but there was an inversion. The core had rotted out, and the presence there was so overwhelmingly wrong that she immediately shied away upon contact. But the aftereffect was almost as strong. She collapsed into a ball of tears, feeling helpless to even remove the energy from her mind even though she wanted it out more than anything. Cutyri wrapped her arms around Ru, and a gentle, steady calm seeped in. "It is not fair," Cutyri agreed quietly. "There is still hope, young one. Will you help us?"

"Yes."

"Fuse will know of the artifacts I speak of. I will send you back to Skae, and you will gather the other Skaeya and

meet Fuse in the Irescan forest as soon as you possibly can.
Your search will begin immediately. Can you do that?"
Ru nodded.

Chapter 23 ★★★ The Challenge

"Shryke, why are we here?"

He ignored Sylph and slouched further down on the wood-slat bench. The mall was fairly busy, it was Friday and not long after the high school got out, so a rogue Blue Star was unlikely to pop up and start a battle. Still, Sylph could see no purpose in being at this particular location.

"Shryke."

"Who's Shryke? My name's Shawn."

Sylph rolled her eyes. To be fair, he was right. "Sylph" and "Shryke" would be too uncommon of names for most people here even though they were based on English words. "The Skaeya won't be here," she said. "They don't get out of school for another hour."

"I know."

"Then why are were here?"

Shryke took a long sip of the soda in his hand. "I don't know why *you're* here. I'm looking for a date."

"What?" Sylph yelled.

Shryke barely gave her a glance. "Look, for one, do you expect me to go running into their school and just take them out in front of all the other students and faculty? Even if you just used your poisons they'd pick you out for a suspicious person, and then our cover would be blown forever. But we're not supposed to go after them in an isolated area either so what do you think we're supposed to do?"

"*Not* be several miles away from them?"

"We can't *stalk* them, that'd look weird too."

Sylph crossed her arms. "You're just making excuses."

"Please. And you just want to suck up to Kestrel. I know you've got a thing for him and as far as I'm concerned you can have him. I don't have to go around all day pretending every idea he has is pure gold and that all his orders make sense."

Sylph gave a strangled, exasperated cry, her face almost as red as her hair. "That is not why -- you're going to be in *big* trouble when Kestrel finds out you've been hanging out here all day doing nothing."

Shryke's eyes widened and he scoffed in mock offense. "Nothing? Surveillance is important."

Sylph followed his gaze to a group of young women peering at shoes through a window. "Not the kind of surveillance you're doing."

"By the way, that's a big if. Kestrel doesn't like being seen in broad daylight, probably a good thing because he doesn't know how to blend in like we do. And even if he got over that for whatever reason, he'd be distracted by that shiny new bookstore at the other end of the mall."

"He would be focused on the *mission*."

Shryke snorted. "You call it focus. I call it obsession."

Sylph pointed a finger inches from his nose. "Listen, scrub. You'd better be willing to be a little more 'obsessed' than you are. Just because you've been with us for a few centuries does not mean you're irreplaceable. And you *know* what it means to be 'replaced.'"

A flash of nervousness crossed his face, but he grinned. "It almost sounds like you care about me."

Sylph resisted any denial, knowing he was both trying to derail and fluster her. "Exactly how much work have you done in the past decade?"

"First of all, maybe I'm not into kidnapping or fighting middle schoolers? Consider that for a minute. It's weird, OK? I know that might be the entire point of the Council making those kids Skaeya, but it's still weird. I *know* Kestrel thinks so because he tried making up all these excuses about why we need to capture these Skaeya instead of killing them. Which by the way, you screwed up."

"Killing Ru was an accident."

"Sorry, what? How does someone 'accidentally' fall onto the end of a naginata? And second, I've done *tons* of work over the past decade. In the past week. I'm super busy like, most of the time."

A cold voice cut in. "Yes, you look absolutely swamped."

Shryke jumped, crushing the soda in his hand and spraying the remains everywhere. Kestrel loomed over him. Unfortunately, just as Shryke had mentioned, he'd made no attempt to blend in with the crowd. He had his usual long black coat and blue hair, which drew several eyes.

"Sylph -- why did you not bring the Skaeya leader to me?"

Sylph looked startled. "There wasn't any point. We can't reform a dead Skaeya."

"She is alive and recovered."

A silence in the group.

"Someone's in trouble," Shryke sang.

Sylph spared him a glare. "But that's not possible! I --
"

Kestrel silenced her with a look. "Do not make assumptions next time."

Sylph shrank, and Shryke just barely suppressed a snicker. Kestrel rounded on him. "I know how long you've been here."

"OK, and?" Shryke wiped the soda off his arms onto his shirt. "Like I was just explaining to Misty here, our operations are pointless right now. Kinda are in general. Harrier should just blow up this planet and then we wouldn't have to worry about it anymore."

"Harrier does not want Skae destroyed."

"Why not?"

"Question him if you like. I will not."

Sylph was not quite over the verbal lash she'd gotten from Kestrel, but she said, "Do you even know how much energy it takes to deconstruct a planet? We don't have it. Only the Council has that capability, because of the system."

There was a sudden, subtle change in Kestrel's expression. A strange thought had crossed his mind, strong, but not enough for him to express. He seemed uneasy. "Return to base," was all he said.

Even Shryke picked up on his mood, which was unusual. The hall to the mall security headquarters was well-hidden between the gaping entryways of a jewelry store and a candy shop. The three of them slipped into one of the empty conference rooms. One by one, they morphed into Lraenu, and used the electrical system to teleport away.

Upon arrival back at the Irescan base, Shryke and Sylph found Kestrel in human form at a window. A continuous, shrill ringing filled the air, distant but just loud enough to jar the ear. "What is that?" Sylph asked.

"*That* is the earth-shaking, bone-chilling, all-consuming sound of pure unadulterated *lytra rage*," Shryke said, shielding one ear. "And I haven't eaten one of the little fluffballs in years, so don't look at me."

Kestrel climbed onto the windowsill. "Fuse."

"Kestrel, no!" Sylph cried. "Get Pi! He's the only one who can --"

"Whoa, whoa," Shryke interrupted. "No. You know the rule. Never pretend we need Pi for anything."

"His assistance will be as unnecessary as it is unwelcome." Kestrel checked his swords, which had fortunately been hidden in the mall. "The bird has called us out. For this, she has waived the protection of the Council's guardian. She is not a fighter, but she is more dangerous to us than the Skaeya."

"But it could be a trap."

"I intend to investigate first. Gather a squadron to follow, but keep your distance. If this goes well, we may have one less of the Council to worry about."

Jayson slammed his hat on the ground. "I told you! I told you the first night, something was wrong, didn't I?"

No one answered, no one even looked at him. The four Skaeya stood in a circle at the edge of Tanager Park. Ru had been reduced to tears explaining, and Colleen was about to join in. She could barely believe what she was saying, on a beautiful warm day like this with a crystalline blue sky, her classmates in the distance on some of the picnic tables, younger kids on the playground, park workers setting up more decorations for the festival and tourists with their cameras. They had no idea how close they were to the end of it all.

"We have to get out of Quarterhill," Colleen said.

"Weren't you *listening?*" Jayson shouted. "The whole *galaxy* is about to be destroyed!"

A mother pushed a stroller past them, either oblivious to what they were saying or thinking they were talking about some game.

"There has to be someone we can talk to? The FBI? The Army?"

"What are they going to do? They know how to get to the moon. The aliens can cross the galaxy like it's nothing."

"Nah, dude, it's just us." Randy's voice was unusually calm. "We're the ones that gotta fight."

"That's your answer for everything," Jayson said.

"Look, if we stay and do nothing, we're dead. Even if we leave the galaxy, the Lraenu could find us. Sooner or later we're going to have to fight 'em if we want to live. This Cutyri lady said we have a chance to prove ourselves and we could save the lives of everyone on Earth in the process."

"You're right," Ru said, "For once."

"Is a week from the end of the world really the right time to be making jokes?" Jayson groaned.

"I can't run," Ru said. "I don't know about you guys, but I couldn't live with knowing I didn't do everything I could to save everyone."

The others were silent, even Jayson, though Randy nodded in fierce agreement.

"Let's put it this way." Ru picked Jayson's cap up from the dirt. "Do you still think you're dreaming?"

"Yeah?"

She handed to cap to him. "Then what do you have to lose?"

Kestrel was unsure of how to approach the bird. As Sylph said, it could very well be a trap. In Lraenu form, his mind was not nearly as sharp, clouded by persistent destructive instinct and suggestibility. Even though he had worked hard to minimize these weaknesses, he knew they would always be there. Ultimately, though, he decided to make his approach as a Lraenu. While Fuse seemed to be used to the Lraenu aura due to frequent exposure, anyone accompanying her would likely not be, a possible advantage for Kestrel. Furthermore, the only attacks that could be made on him as a Lraenu would be to force him *out* of Lraenu form or to capture him. He wished he knew if Fuse was alone – the ability to sense living things was granted to his enemies via the system, but the Lraenu did not have it and likely would not unless the System was fully infiltrated. Harrier's plan was not to keep the System at all.

In any case, there was no use in trying to sneak up on Fuse. Not only would any Accilean know if he was near, his physical appearance would likely give him away. He had several more tails than most of the other Lraenu, a yellowish-white hue and lantern-gold eyes, all of which glowed. The palm forest was full of glowing things, but not like him. He knew he had no element of surprise. What he did not expect was Fuse to launch straight at him the moment he was in sight. The bird was quick enough to strike just above the eye and bounce off. Kestrel would have been amused if he wasn't acutely aware that something about the situation was very wrong.

"I won't let you destroy this galaxy," Fuse growled.

"I hardly see how *you* can do anything about us. You can't even stand the sound of my voice." Kestrel did have to admit he had a little admiration for how steady the bird's flight was, even though she was cringing hard. "But we're not destroying your galaxy. We're simply neutralizing the hold the system has on it."

"Show me your true form!"

"I have no reason to."

Fuse divebombed him again, but this time Kestrel was ready. He dodged and tried to grab her with one of his tails, but her feathers were too slippery. Again he tried, this time with more tails at once, and missed. He needed all his concentration just to keep track of where Fuse was. On top of that, the more he fought, the more the destructive influence of his Lraenu form seeped into his mind. It was a rage, pure fury that this bird even dared to exist, and Kestrel did not have anyone above him in command to rein that instinct in. If he was not careful, the instinct would completely take over his mind.

Something changed. A thread of light, from the distant gatestone, then a bar. So he would be outnumbered soon, once whoever was coming through caught up to them. Who would it be?

Fuse had not yet noticed the stone's activation, but she did when one of the arrivals called out her name. She stopped, and Kestrel lashed out with a tail. The little bird went tumbling through the air and landed in the sand in a burst of feathers. A second later her human form appeared, face-down in the sand.

"We have to help," a small voice said.

Kestrel froze in mid-air. That voice had been in English, a child's voice. It had to be the Skaeya. He saw the four of them near the edge of the stone, still, uncertain. Sylph had given him all of their names and descriptions, but it was a shock to see such small humans armed with Accilean energy, and the only thing that kept him from rushing at them with full force in accordance with the building anger inside him. It distracted him enough that he didn't notice Fuse rise, and the world tumbled when she landed a punch.

He just barely stopped himself from charging and wiping them out in one swoop. The sheer amount of Accilean energy surrounding the lot of them brought him to a level of rage he hadn't felt in years. It took all his mental strength to keep himself still, focused.

The smallest of the group – Randy, Sylph said his name was – was tensed, fists clenched, ready to run right into the fight. The two girls watched with wide eyes. There was a strange, detached calm in the other boy's expression. "Why is Fuse fighting?" Ru asked faintly.

"*Hello?!*" Randy yelled. "Do you see that marshmallow octopus trying to kill her?"

"No, no!" Ru grabbed his sleeve. "Don't you remember the first night we were here? Jayson asked Fuse why she didn't fight. She said she wasn't allowed to!"

"Oh yeah, I'm sure the rules matter a whole lot when a monster's trying to *murder* you," Randy jerked away from her.

So they knew the rule, but not Fuse's purpose for being here. Kestrel tried to reason through it. If the Skaeya didn't know what was happening, the Council might not know either. And the Council's seemingly omniscient guardian was nowhere to be found, so likely Fuse had challenged him on her own. But why?

"Does she not believe in us anymore?" Ru asked, to no one.

Why Fuse would ever believe in them in the first place was a mystery to Kestrel. Even if they hadn't been children, they would have been very new. He was going to speak again, but Randy dashed forward. Green light burst from his fist, a beacon of pure Accilean energy. The fury that Kestrel had struggled to contain surged and broke free.

"Skaeya, no! Run!" Fuse shouted.

Randy skidded to a halt. "What?"

"Go back home!"

Before Kestrel knew it, he was flying towards them with the intent of obliterating them. The only way he could think to slow himself down and save his directive was to turn back into human form. Rust-colored negative light dimmed the air around him as he drew closer. As he did, he noticed Colleen go still, extremely pale, a look of pure horror on her face. And then – anger. Anger? Wasn't she supposed to be the timid one? Against all that Sylph had reported to him, she was the first one that rose up to meet him. She just barely missed Fuse, and headed straight at Kestrel, hands splayed out in front of her. Unfortunately for her, her awkward flight path was easy to read. He dodged her arms at the last moment, seized her by the throat with his newly-formed hands, and dispelled the bulk of the Laenu rage by hurling her at the ground. She bounced once and lay still. He put his sword to her throat. "Colleen, NO!" Ru screamed.

She tried to fly at him next, but Fuse grabbed her arm and set her firmly on the ground. "Back off, Kestrel," Fuse threatened. "Leave her alone."

"You started this," Kestrel said. "I only meant to have a discussion."

Jayson inched closer to Fuse. "That's not just another Laenu, is it?"

"No. This is the Laenu High Commander." Fuse bared her teeth. "The four of you need to leave. *Now.*"

Before any of them could take a step, Kestrel disappeared in a flash of negative light and reappeared between the Skaeya and the stone. Green light flared around Randy's fist. "Out of the way!"

Kestrel shook his head solemnly. "Crash," he said with perfect Accilean pronunciation, "won't do you any good. Even if you were skilled enough to catch me with it."

"I said *move!*"

Kestrel easily deflected the glowing punch, which had no effect on his human form, and in one smooth motion, grabbed Randy by the arm and hurled him towards the others. It knocked Jayson down and both boys went rolling.

"*Stop!*" Ru stood tall. "You and your Raenu have to quit messing everything up or the Council's going to destroy us all!"

Kestrel gave her a critical look. "What do you mean?"

"The Angel has appeared," Fuse growled. "Why do you think I called you out?"

"The Angel" meant nothing to Kestrel, but suddenly everything else clicked.

It *was* desperation on their part. They did have the power to destroy the planet, let alone the galaxy. And the Caere, suddenly attacking all Lraenu unprovoked, using its precious energy and threatening to expose the truth to all the unawakened Skaeyans? What would be the point of hiding if Skae was about to be destroyed?

He stared at Ru. "They told you the Lraenu are 'corrupting' your world." Anger began to seep back in, and lightning sparked in the air around him. The Skaeya and Fuse backed up, Ru all the way to Colleen, who was still lying lifeless in the sand. "Yet they are the ones who force all their inhabitants into the system, send their *children* unprepared into battle, and threaten to destroy an entire galaxy because they cannot have complete control over it? The Accileans are not fit for such power. We will *not* surrender to them!”

He knew it was a mistake, but the new revelation combined with the remnants of destructive Lraenu instinct took over again. He raised his blade above his head, and a single bolt of lightning flashed through the air. It was all that was needed to entirely level the Accileans.

Fortunately they seemed to still be alive; they were all moving, though not much. Not one returned to their feet. He took a moment to clear his head, reminding himself of his intent, and calmly walked towards the leader. Glazed blue eyes stared up at him. He was unsure if she could actually see him. "Disarm and surrender your talisman," he commanded.

"W-what?" she whispered. “Disarm?”

"Return to your normal form. This entire battle is unnecessary, and we have much to discuss. However, I cannot let a Skaeya live. Surrender your power and I will spare you. What more, I will give you the truths the Accileans will not."

“Fuse? What is he talking about?”

"Nothing." Fuse's voice was hoarse. “You know what we know now.”

“Do I sense mistrust here?” Kestrel said. “It appears that the bird was deceitful before. Why should you believe her?”

“I –”

“Why does he need you to give up your power if he just wants to talk?” Fuse said, louder.

Kestrel bristled at the sound of her voice. "Quiet!" he barked. Lightning bolts shimmered around his hand. "The Accileans have said *enough*!"

In the moment just before he sent it, he heard Ru speak. He paid no mind to her at first, until he noticed the glow. Blue light sparked from her pendant, and her glazed eyes were now focused sharply, swimming in the same glow. She took a deep breath.

"I WON'T LET YOU TURN THE SKY AGAINST ME!" she screamed.

In Accilean.

Kestrel rerouted the lightning towards Ru. It struck him instead. He was blown off clean off his feet. Another bolt flashed, lightning he did not summon, followed closely by an explosive crackle of thunder.

Both Kestrel and Ru slowly regained their footing. Churning light surrounded Ru, as did a sudden gale that stole his breath and nearly took him down again. A maelstrom of blue meteors and greenish clouds swirled up around her. She curled her fists, and the storm exploded outwards, temporarily blinding him. When he could see again, he knew the danger was real.

The only thing that had remained the same about Ru was the blue headband with tails, flapping wildly in the wind that encircled her. She now wore shimmering, deep blue armor. A seal with the four-winged symbol of the Skaeya was held at her chest by two sashes. She wore gloves with gauntlets and metallic boots, and her eyes were alight with the blazing blue of a midday sky. She pointed at him with a certainty and intent he would have never expected to see from someone so young, and for the first time in ages, he felt something beyond simple wariness, beyond a challenge, something bigger. It could have been fear.

Another deafening boom drew his attention to the sky. The clouds were twisting, a deep mass of blue-green,

swimming with lightning. Ru spoke another Accilean word --
a command, unheard over the roar of the wind, and raised
her pointed finger to the sky. The sky understood and
obeyed.

Kestrel made one feeble, last-ditch effort to launch an
attack. The lightning he sent immediately turned back on him
again, and the shock made him lose track of all that was
happening. The last thing he saw was Ru engulfed by a
tornado, and an uprooted palm tree sailing through the air
towards him.

Chapter 24 ★★★ An Awakening

The High Commander never hit the ground. There was a flash of negative light, and briefly Ru saw Sylph catch him, a split-second glare in her direction before flashing away again. Just as quickly as it set in, the tornado gusted away, the clouds drifted back to sleep with a quiet rumble of thunder. Stars glimmered through the swaying trees, leaves quit their spin and rained to the ground. At last, the glow peeled off Ru in wisps, only leaving her eyes with an unearthly skylight shine.

The others, shaken and aching, slowly stood.

"What -- what was that?" Jayson asked.

"Bet you couldn't do it again," Randy said.

Ru, who had been in something of an anger-fueled daze, had no answer. She was checking her new armor, puzzled over the change. Fuse ran to Ru, breathless. "That was an awakening of an Axle! You are awakened!" Her hand flew to her mouth, and she laughed. "The galaxy -- we could have a chance now. Yes! You could save it! We could save it!"

Ru's face lit up. "We can?"

"Hey, wait a second!" Randy yelled. "How come *she* gets armor! I should get some if I have *light* for a power!"

Beyond him, Ru saw Colleen stir on the ground. Ru blew past everyone and screeched to a halt next to her friend, tossing up a cloud of sand. "Colleen! You OK?!"

Colleen stared with bleary eyes, confused, but gasped and smiled when she laid eyes on Fuse. "You're alive," she breathed. "What happened?"

"She should probably see a doctor," Jayson said. "We all should. We got struck by lightning, didn't we?"

"You'll be healed once you turn back to your normal forms," Fuse explained.

"Yeah, and I ain't going anywhere 'til I get my armor!" Randy screeched.

Jayson snorted a laugh. "You gotta earn it, mooch!"

A quick check revealed that there were no more Lraenu in the vicinity, and the Skaeya moved on to the Council's complex. Ru had vague memories of the complex and the actual people there, but this was the first time she had seen this endless hall of mirrors clearly, and the true scope of all the alien leaders who had been near. Two of them could not be seen at all; she only knew they were there because of the System, and that the one named Veah was extremely vocal.

Once inside the complex, Randy immediately tried to see how far he could slide across the highly-polished floor before Jayson grabbed him and firmly placed him back with the group. Colleen wedged herself close to Fuse, and Ru stayed nearby.

"Why *did* you attack the High Commander?" Ru asked her, after Colleen had been caught up on the part of the fight she'd missed. "I would have never thought you'd fight first."

Colleen beamed, and she stumbled all over herself trying to explain. At last, she said, "It was that dream! The High Commander was the one who killed Fuse. Remember I told you he was a red star and he came out of that? That's what I saw! But I stopped it!"

"Oh, wow! You did!" Ru cheered, wrapping her in a hug. "You totally did!"

They quieted as they entered the heartroom, though Randy strode in first with his fists raised. "Hey, Area 51!

Shawn "Shryke" Lanius

Birthday: Unknown
(age ~500 years)
Species: Lraenu
Homeworld: Unknown

Shryke is the Lraenu expert on Earth cultures. He monitors the planet for unusual activity concerning the Accileans, and usually works in tandem with Sylph to hunt down Skaeya. In truth, Shryke dislikes working for the Lraenu and has built himself an entire alternate life on Earth. As Shawn, he studied to be a programmer, but is now rising to fame as the lead singer of a popular local band. His tendency to take the easy way out of everything has given him a bad reputation, and he is not above lying and sacrificing others to get his way, but most people overlook this side of him due to his charm, quick wit, and good looks.

Misty "Sylph" Elesti

Birthday: Unknown
(age ~500 years)
Species: Lraenu
Homeworld:
Unknown

Sylph's sole task is to
seek and destroy
Skaeya, which she
handles with precision
and aloofness. She is

somewhat protective of her fellow Lraenu, but has a short
temper and often resorts to violence to get what she wants.
She has almost as good a grip on American culture as Shryke,
and is very effective at using this knowledge in her missions.
Unlike Shryke, she hates spending long periods of time on
Earth. She is competitive and does not have much respect for
authority – Kestrel is the only Lraenian commander she
obeys unconditionally.